-27-06

DATE DUE

MAR 2 7 2006	
JUL 1 3 2006	
ILL 2007	
ILL 2007	

Landon Snow

and the Shadows of Malus Quidam

R. K. MORTENSON

BARBOUR
PUBLISHING

Landon Snow

Snow

and the Shadows of Malus Quidam

© 2006 by R. K. Mortenson

ISBN 1-59789-044-8

All scripture quotations are taken from the King James Version of the Bible.

This book is a work of fiction. Names, characters, places, and incidents are either products of the author's imagination or used fictitiously. Any similarity to actual people, organizations, and/or events is purely coincidental.

Cover and interior illustrations by Cory Godbey, Portland Studios.
    www.portlandstudios.com
Cover design by DogEared Design, llc.

Published by Barbour Publishing, Inc., P.O. Box 719, Uhrichsville, Ohio 44683
www.barbourbooks.com

Our mission is to publish and distribute inspirational products offering exceptional value and biblical encouragement to the masses.

ecpa Member of the
Evangelical Christian
Publishers Association

Printed in the United States of America.
5 4 3 2 1

Dedication

This is for my wife, Betsy.
Thank you for reflecting a greater Light.

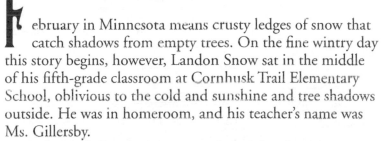

Chapter One

February in Minnesota means crusty ledges of snow that catch shadows from empty trees. On the fine wintry day this story begins, however, Landon Snow sat in the middle of his fifth-grade classroom at Cornhusk Trail Elementary School, oblivious to the cold and sunshine and tree shadows outside. He was in homeroom, and his teacher's name was Ms. Gillersby.

Valentine's Day had just passed, and the classroom was festooned in pink, white, and red. Chains of hearts circled the room, and one giant red construction-paper heart bloomed behind the calendar on the wall. A black arrow pierced the heart at an angle, going in through one rounded lobe and coming out near the point at the bottom.

Landon stared at the arrow, and his heart began to race. He was remembering a wild ride through a forest on horseback. An elflike creature called an Odd fired a hail of arrows as Landon and his horse friend, Melech, raced for their lives. No matter how far they ran, the arrows kept coming. The Odd who was shooting at them, Landon later learned, was named Maple Tree Max, or Long Shot. Max had quite a range, but only one of every hundred of his shots found its mark. Maple Tree Max was the man on the perimeter, the Hundred-to-One Odd. . . .

"Landon Snow, are you paying attention?"

Landon nearly shouted, "Ho, Ludo!" before he checked himself and realized where he was. A figure loomed before him, her hands on her hips, her lips pursed in a disapproving frown.

"Yes, Ms. Gillersby." The lie slipped out before Landon could stop it.

"Well then, what is the answer?" Her scowl opened like a flower into a broad questioning look.

Blood rushed into Landon's face as he heard a couple of kids snicker behind him. The teacher gave them a sharp glance, and the room became quiet except for the soft tick of the clock. *Ticktock.* Landon sneaked a peek at it. *Ticktock.* The bell wouldn't ring for another five minutes. He sighed. It was too long to wait.

What was the question? Should he ask and reveal his lie? Or should he take a blind stab at it? Before his mind totally clouded, Landon blurted the first thing that popped into it.

"Twenty-one," he said feigning confidence.

The classroom fell apart, and Ms. Gillersby's face shrank as if she'd just bit into a lemon. She quickly swiveled her head, quieting every laughing student with her eyes. Then she settled her gaze on Landon so long he could hear blood marching in his ears with the rhythm of the clock.

Ticktock.

Ticktock.

"No, Mr. Snow. Our sixteenth president was not Twenty-one." Her eyes briefly darted to squelch any giggles. "Can anyone tell me who was the sixteenth president of the United States?"

A hand shot up.

"Yes, Cammie?"

"Abraham Lincoln."

"Very good." Ms. Gillersby smiled at her star pupil and then glared at Landon before turning and striding to the front of the room. "Each year in February we celebrate President's Day in honor of George Washington and Abraham Lincoln. . . ."

Her voice droned away as Landon looked at a picture of the sixteenth president that was made of cut pieces of white and black paper. The largest piece was his top hat. The only person Landon had ever seen wear a top hat in real life was a sprightly sprig of a fellow named Ludo. He was the leader of the Odds and the reader of the Coin, which Landon had seen hoisted into the night sky from the center of the Echoing Green.

As the bell buzzed, Landon was jolted back into the classroom. Ms. Gillersby wished everyone a happy President's Day weekend, and then she stopped Landon on his way out.

"Are you okay, Landon?" said his teacher, shifting into her less-stern-between-classes mode. "You seemed distracted today."

"Yeah," said Landon, trying not to act impatiently. "I'm fine, just excited for our trip."

"Oh? And where are you going?"

"We're going to Button Up to see my grandparents."

"Button Up—where the big library is, right?"

"Yeah!" Landon's eyes grew wide despite himself. He was not only distracted; he was excited. The greatest adventure he had ever known had started—and ended—in Button Up. "Can I go now, Ms. Gillersby? I still need to pack."

"Certainly. Have a good trip."

"Thanks," said Landon, and over his shoulder he added, "Sorry. . . ." This was for being distracted in class, but because he was already halfway to his locker when he said it, the apology seemed to get lost in the hubbub of the hallway.

On the bus ride home, Landon thought about Grandpa Karl's study and the swinging bookcase and the secret tunnel and the first part of the Auctor's Riddle on Bartholomew G. Benneford's rowboat tombstone.

The bus hit a bump, and Landon swallowed with a gulp. As excited as he was to see his grandparents and visit the BUL (Button Up Library), he was also a little nervous and sad. What if he could never go back to the forest again? Then he would not see the friends he had made there. The foolish Odd named Hardy, who wasn't so foolish after all. The old man Vates and his signs and poems and messages. The girl Ditty, who literally snapped Landon from Ludo's enchanting spell. And (a lump formed in his throat) Melech, his noble steed.

Melech wasn't Landon's horse by ownership or anything. When Landon thought of him as *his horse* or *his noble steed*, it was like saying *his friend*. A friend who happened to be a horse.

Landon really wanted to see him again. And the others, too. As time had passed, drifting from his birthday in early

October to Halloween and then Thanksgiving and right on through Christmas, New Year's, and now Valentine's Day. . .well, the whole thing seemed more and more like a dream. Landon had seen Grandpa Karl and Grandma Alice over Christmas, but they had come down to Minneapolis for the visit. This would be Landon's first time back in Button Up since his birthday in October.

Time, of course, is measured best by holidays. Until this year, this very weekend, Landon had hardly cared about President's Day. It hadn't seemed a real holiday, to be quite honest, even though they got the day off from school. (And this was only because it happened to coincide with a teachers' workshop.) The very best holidays involved presents, of course. These would be Christmas and one's birthday. The next best involved candy, to include Easter (chocolate eggs and bunnies), Halloween (chocolate bars and candy corn), and even Valentine's Day (chocolate hearts and hard candy hearts with silly red phrases). Next would be the Fourth of July (fireworks), New Year's (stay up late and watch TV), and Thanksgiving (turkey, stuffing, pumpkin pie, and football). But President's Day? What was so great about President's Day?

Well, it meant the Snow family was headed up north, so just maybe another adventure might be in store for Landon. That would definitely move President's Day up on his holiday list.

Landon's sister Holly, a fourth grader who was less than a year younger than him (and never let him forget it), sidled alongside him as they started walking from the bus stop.

"I hear you like Cammie Dewdrop," she said.

Landon took several brisk steps, breathing in the icy air,

before he realized what Holly had said. Without breaking stride he said, "Who told you that?"

"Cammie did," Holly said in a singsong. "She said you gave her a Valentine."

Landon stopped in his tracks. "I gave *everyone* a Valentine." He continued crunching through the hard-packed snow. When he reached the front door to his house, he held the handle with his gloved hand and muttered as if Holly wasn't there. "Besides, my real Valentine is saved for somebody else."

Uh, oh. As soon as he said it, Holly leaned in with narrow, piercing eyes.

"Who?" she asked, pushing against the door. "Who is she? Danielle? Emma? Madeline? *Who?*"

Landon shook his head and puffed out a thick cloud of frosty breath. "You don't *know* her, Holly. Let go of the door."

"You have to tell me, or I'm going to tell Cammie it *is* her."

"That's not fair," said Landon. "And that would be lying."

"Well, you lied to Ms. Gillersby today." Holly narrowed her eyes and smiled with thin, tight lips.

How did she know this stuff? "I did not. I just got the answer wrong. Besides, you weren't even there. Who told you?"

Holly laughed. "You didn't see me sitting by her on the bus, did you?"

Landon tilted his head. "Who?" He tugged on the door, but Holly leaned against it harder.

"Cammie! Wow, you really *are* distracted, Landon. You have to tell me."

Landon groaned. Despite being in the fourth grade, Holly had somehow managed to weasel her way into friendships with a lot of his fifth-grade classmates. At least all the girl classmates. This had often put him at a disadvantage, as he had no inside "spies" watching Holly in her classes. Not that he really wanted any.

"Come on, Holly. It's cold, and we've got to pack."

"I packed last night, and if you don't tell me who you're in love with, I'm telling Mom and Dad you lied to your teacher."

Landon blew a stream of vapor like a chimney. His lungs felt like they were about to burst from the icy air. As much as he didn't want to tell his sister about the girl whom he thought about most often (he wasn't quite in love with her, however—that was pushing it rather far), something inside him suddenly *did* want to tell her. He wanted to share not only about the girl, but *everything* that had happened to him that wondrous night he fell into the *Book of Meanings* at the Button Up Library.

"Her name's Ditty," he said finally, feeling relief and disgust for giving in to his sister. "Anyway, you don't know her."

Holly frowned, searching Landon's face. Then she smiled and burst out laughing. "Ditty? What kind of a dumb name is that?" She clapped her hands and chanted, "Landon loves Ditty, Landon loves Dit—"

But her chant was cut off as Landon yanked the door open, sending Holly sprawling from the step and into the snow.

"She's not dumb," said Landon glaring. "It's not her fault that she can't read. And she's probably a lot smarter than you." Landon was panting uncontrollably and clenching his fists, surprised by his own anger.

Holly stared back at him, sitting awkwardly in the snow with her knees jutting up. "She can't *read*? How old is she,

Landon?" She didn't look hurt or angry, only curious and surprised.

Landon tried to control himself. He looked down at the powdery snow on the step. "I—I don't know. I don't even know how ages work there." His mind was beginning to spin. He had never talked with anyone about this. It felt a little weird. So far it had been his special secret.

Holly was getting up and brushing herself off, all the while looking askance at her brother. "How ages work *where*, Landon?" She stood before the step, out of reach from the door. "What in the world are you talking about?"

Landon looked at her, and he felt a smile lifting his face. "Not *what*. *Where*. The question is *where* in the world am I talking about. I'll tell you everything," Landon added, "on the way."

Holly nodded, and they went inside so Landon could pack.

The youngest Snow family member—Bridget—had the first bench in the SUV all to herself, and she was sprawled out and hidden from Landon's and Holly's view as they sat together in the backseat. Bridget was sleeping even though she had voted for the movie that was playing on the DVD player.

Landon and Holly paid the movie no heed. Landon did notice his mother peeking back at them every now and then with a bemused smirk on her face. The reasons for his mother's expression, Landon figured, were probably: (1) nobody was watching the corny movie, (2) he and Holly were sitting together in the backseat (Landon usually fought for the seat and got it all to himself for these trips), and (3) because he—not Holly—was doing all the talking and Holly was doing all the listening. His mom was probably curious about what he could be telling Holly that kept her from talking and from counting objects outside.

Holly loved math, and often she counted things merely for the sake of counting them. Usually she'd report her totals at the end of the trip. On their last trip to Button Up, she had counted water towers and Dairy Queens, of all things. Though Holly wasn't counting or making comments about things out loud, Landon did notice her glancing at the road and silently tallying the hash marks as their car gobbled them up. Holly just couldn't help it. Still, she was listening to his story and at certain parts making faces that expressed wonder or alarm or mild fear. Mostly, however, she seemed to express doubt and skepticism.

"So," Holly said, interrupting Landon at one point, "you're saying the *Book of Meanings* grew bigger than. . .than a *building*? And then you *climbed it*?"

Another time she said, "The giant knight piece picked you up and carried you to the edge of this board place, and then you jumped together, and it turned into a *horse*?"

So it went throughout Landon's tale. When he finally reached the end, Holly said, "And there you were standing outside Grandma and Grandpa's, after you'd stepped out from—what's his name? Vates?—after stepping out from Vates's place in the hillside?"

Landon nodded. He felt exhausted. It had taken him nearly two hours to tell his story. Tired as he was, there was also great joy and relief for finally having shared his adventures. What a fantastic journey it had been!

"Wow," said Holly, staring out the windshield and counting road stripes.

Landon looked at her. It wasn't the response he'd been hoping for. "Wow, what?" he said finally, though it was tiring just to ask. He preferred not having to ask questions, figuring things out on his own. But he couldn't figure out Holly's deadpan reaction.

"Well, wow, big brother," she said, turning her head and swishing her straight blond hair. "I mean, you made up all that to tell me you don't like Cammie Dewdrop. I mean, wow, I am impressed. You've got more imagination than I'd—"

"What?" he shouted.

Landon's mom turned, and he lowered his voice. "What do you mean, Holly? You think I made that stuff up? About the Bible's pages turning and the bookcase opening and—and. . ." It was hard to speak through all his agitation and bewilderment. "And everything? Ditty is real. And so is Vates and Hardy and Ludo and"—a lump formed in his throat—"and Melech."

Did she really not believe him? Suddenly he wished he hadn't opened his big mouth after all. His adventure was better as a secret that seemed like a dream than as a shared story that only met disbelief.

Holly switched her gaze from the road to the screen that was flipped down from the ceiling. The movie's credits were scrolling upward. She appeared to be counting the names.

Landon wanted to scream or at least make Holly sit in front with Bridget where she belonged. What a waste of time this had been. He would never confide in her again, that was for sure. He looked out his window to the white-frosted evergreens and the fields of snow that lay spread like blank pages in a huge, vast book. "It was real," he muttered to himself. "And Ludo's tree was bigger than all those trees put together."

What Landon hadn't told Holly was that Vates had said he probably could return to their land again if he really wanted to. Landon's desire to do so was growing, yet he couldn't help but wonder how he would get back. He'd left Melech and Ditty and Hardy with Vates in the hill. Would he have to go back through the *Book of Meanings* again? And into the Quality Control room? And onto the giant chessboard? Landon swallowed anxiously at the thought of the dark king. He didn't want to have to face him again. Besides that, Melech was no longer on the board, so if Landon got stuck there again, who would help him? Would another piece come to his rescue?

Landon was still lost in his thoughts when he felt something nudge his arm. It was Holly. The video screen was blank. The movie credits were done. What did Holly want now? To switch places with him so she could better count the telephone poles, which ran along his side of the road?

"There's one way you can prove it," she said quietly. Landon studied his sister's face, ready to tell her to brush off if she was only kidding around. She appeared to be earnest.

"What's that?" he said, not getting his hope up.

"You said you took Grandma and Grandpa's flashlight, right? That it fell and broke down in that, uh, tunnel you said you went through underground?"

Slowly Landon nodded.

"Well, if the flashlight's gone and Grandma and Grandpa don't know where it is, I might believe you. *Might*," she added for emphasis.

"No, Holly," said Landon, "you *will* believe me. Because I'm not making it up. You'll get to see for yourself that this"—he motioned to the outside world—"isn't all there is. There's more, much more than even I have seen. I've only caught a glimpse of a vision, a tiny part of a dream that's not made up but is even more real than real."

The words sounded like nonsense even to him, yet Holly seemed to take them in. "More real than real," she said. "I want to see this place."

Landon smiled. Besides smiling at his sister, he was smiling at the thought of two things he'd packed into his travel bag. One was a hard plastic flashlight with a shatterproof lens and a wrist strap. The other was his Bible, which Grandpa Karl and Grandma Alice had given him for his eleventh birthday.

Chapter Two

Grandma Alice's dinner tasted good. The fire in the fireplace blazed hot and bright. Everyone huddled under blankets as Grandpa Karl told a story about a Viking expedition off the coast of Norway. Landon's family was glad to be inside a warm, dry house rather than aboard a rickety ship being thrown about upon icy waves. Landon and Holly found themselves glancing at each other during the stormy and dangerous parts. A glimmer shone in their eyes that came from more than the glow of the fire.

When the story ended, Bridget asked, "Were the Vikings good guys or bad guys?"

Grandpa Karl gave his beard a gentle tug. "Well," he said, "I presume they were a bit of both. Just like all of us, really. I mean, God created us good, and He wants us to be good, but sometimes, well, we slip up. Before God, we have all sinned. There was only one man who was truly and totally good, through and through."

"That was Jesus, right?" asked Bridget.

Grandpa Karl smiled. "That was Jesus. So, Bridget, the Vikings did do some bad and terrible things. There's no excusing that. But I don't know that I'd say they were all bad and terrible men." He paused and sighed. "How do I put it? We all struggle with good and bad, and so we all need Jesus. How's that?"

Bridget nodded. "That's good."

Landon thought of lying to his teacher, saying he'd been paying attention when he hadn't been. He felt a small stab in his heart and looked toward the fire.

A draft from somewhere caused the blaze to flare. The flames stretched and curled almost like a large yellow flickering hand. Landon turned and noticed lines of shadow shifting and darkening across his grandfather's face. The shadow came from the fireplace grille and formed horizontal bars spilling over Grandpa Karl that made it appear he was trapped inside a crooked, shadowy jail cell. The lines had been there before, but had it not been for that sudden gust of flame, Landon probably wouldn't have noticed them. A shadow line rested across his own arm, as well. It wavered ever so slightly as the fire glimmered and popped. Landon brushed at it, but of course this only caused the shadow to fall across his brushing hand.

Grandpa Karl stood. "So tomorrow, it's off to the library, eh? And maybe some tobogganing down the hill for you kids later on?"

"Yeah!" Bridget's cheer promptly turned into a big, wide yawn. "Sliding, Holly!" She looked at her sister. "Can I go on the big inner tube, Grandpa?"

Grandpa Karl laughed. "Sure, you can all go on there, as

long as you steer clear of those trees."

"We don't want any mishaps or accidents for *anyone* during your visit this time," said Grandma Alice giving Grandpa Karl a look. "Right, dear?"

Landon's father chimed in. "He's not working on that jalopy tonight. Oh no. I am *not* getting up for a midnight drive to Brainerd. I plan to stay snug under the covers until I smell either coffee or eggs in the morning."

"Or pancakes?" Grandma Alice raised her eyebrows.

"Or pancakes." Landon's dad nodded. "Now the sooner we get to bed, the sooner we'll smell breakfast. Up you go, girls. Good night, Landon."

Landon thanked Grandma for supper and Grandpa for the story. He said good night to everyone and headed for Grandpa Karl's study, where his sleeping bag was rolled out on the sofa. But he paused near the stairs and glanced up. Holly was climbing slowly, feigning drowsiness, pulling herself up with the banister. Even Bridget passed her on the way up. Landon noted that the second step from the top gave a groaning creak. He hoped Holly noticed as well so she would skip it on her way back down, which, according to plan, would be in another hour and ten minutes.

Come on, Holly, he thought. *Remember the signal!*

Holly paused with her foot on the creaky step. She tamped it twice—*errk, errk*—as if to show she was aware of its temperament. Then she glanced quickly toward the hallway, caught Landon's eye, and blinked twice. Landon repeated the gesture back to her—blink, blink—and retreated to Grandpa Karl's study to wait. His heart already was beginning to pound with anticipation.

An hour and ten minutes had never passed so slowly. This was worse than waiting to get up Christmas morning to open presents. To fill the time, Landon checked the large bookcase for hinges or other mechanisms that could explain its silent swinging movement last October. Of course, he had looked back then, too. Again, his search proved fruitless. The bookcase was as heavy and solid as could be. Nothing rested along its back edges except a few clinging strands of cobweb.

That investigation only lasted ten minutes. There was still an hour to kill. Landon checked the flashlight. *Click*—it worked. He then took out his old gray leather Bible, which had presumably been much blacker and shinier in Bartholomew G. Benneford's day. Now it was as wrinkly as elephant skin, and the slightly yellowed pages felt almost as thin and delicate as tissue paper.

Landon opened the cover to reveal the spidery handwriting inside: *Ex Libris B. G. B.*

Ex libris was Latin for *from the library of*, and it struck Landon that it was this book that had also led him to Bartholomew's library that fantastic night. Would it do it again? He flipped eagerly to the pages with the under-lined passages that had triggered the portal: Joel 2:28 and Acts 2:2. "Visions and dreams," Landon said softly, pretending not to be watching the bookcase out of the corner of his eye. "Visions and dreams!" He faced the bookcase and made a windy, blowing sound through his lips. He even flapped his arms. It was useless, and he felt a little silly, not to mention out of breath.

Landon sighed and carried the Bible to the sofa, where he sat down. He thought about what he had learned from

Vates and the Auctor's Riddle—that he wasn't here by
chance and that life wasn't an accident. He had been born
for a reason, and his purpose was to try and get to know the
Auctor. *Auctor* was Latin for "author" or "creator." And the
Author and Creator of life, of course, was God.

Landon was pondering this as he flipped through the
pages of the Bible. Old Bart had been quite busy with his
pen and ruler. Underlined passages stood out everywhere.
Landon's eyelids began to feel heavy, and at one point, as
he found his chin dipping suddenly toward his chest, he
wondered why on earth he was still up when he could very
well be snuggled inside his sleeping bag with the light off.
He was just thinking of changing into his pajamas when he
heard a tapping on the door.

Landon sat up. "Who is it?" he said quickly. Had he
actually fallen asleep?

The doorknob began turning, and Landon stood and set
the Bible on the sofa and reached for his flashlight. He moved
quietly to the backside of the door, raised the flashlight, and
waited. A head of white hair appeared, swishing back and
forth. It was a ghost! Trembling, Landon didn't know whether
to attack the apparition with the flashlight or try to squish
it with the door. Then it moved into the room and turned
toward him.

"Augh!" Landon cried.

"Shh!" said the ghost, who looked startlingly like his sister
Holly. "Do you want to wake everyone? What are you doing
with that flashlight?"

Landon brought the flashlight down, panting. "I forgot. I
mean, I thought you might be something else."

Holly peered at him askance. "Did you fall asleep on me?" She shook her head. "And you're surprised I don't believe your story. Anyway, it's a good thing you have your flashlight. You might want your jacket, too."

"What? Why?" Landon felt a little embarrassed that he'd drifted off. The plan was now coming back to him, although he wasn't sure why he'd need his jacket.

"I looked in the drawer, Landon. Grandpa's flashlight isn't there. At least not the old metal one. There's a brand-new one in there, kind of like yours. So either you were telling the truth about the old one, or Grandpa just lost it. Either way, it might be fun to try to find it. Are you ready to go adventuring?"

Landon stared speechlessly as his sister pulled her knit cap over her head and flung the tasseled ball to one side. She had on her jacket, and he noticed her mittens sticking out from a pocket.

"Why are you all dressed up?" he said. "We're not going outside."

"Oh, come on, Landon. It will be fun. I didn't wait up this late for nothing. We might as well do something, at least pretend."

"But. . ." He was at a loss. She obviously still didn't believe him. She wanted to go outside to look for the flashlight, when it actually lay at the bottom of the mysterious dark stairway at the end of the tunnel. Landon turned toward the bookcase. Was it worth the bother to try telling her again? How a draft had blown in from nowhere and riffled the pages in the Bible and the bookcase had opened. . .on its own?

Just then, something caught Landon's eye along the floor

near the bookcase. He stared and waited. What was it he had seen? "Did you see that?" he whispered.

"See what? Come on, get your jacket on."

Landon gave his sister a squinty glance. "Wait. I saw something move." He checked his flashlight to make sure it was off, and then he slowly scanned the room. He studied the bookcase and then looked back at the baseboard. He pointed. "It was down there."

Holly bobbed her head side to side. "I don't see anything, Landon." Her head stopped moving. "Except. . .that." She pointed, too, and her mouth was hanging open. "What *is* that?"

It was moving again, inching its way toward the bookcase. When it was still, it appeared to be a dark smudge or a stain, so it was nearly invisible. But as it crept silently along, Landon realized what he was looking at, though he couldn't explain how it was there. "It's a shadow," he whispered.

As if it had heard him or knew it was being watched, the shadow stopped. Holding his breath, Landon cautiously took a step nearer. The shadow, which had been a nondescript oblong shape, collapsed to a large dot and then stretched into a line and wriggled snakelike toward the bookcase. Fearing it would disappear before he really got a good look at it, Landon raised his flashlight, aimed, and clicked. The beam caught the shadow in a glowing circle. But only for an instant. The shadow zipped like lightning to the edge of the bookcase and disappeared, apparently slipping behind it.

Landon shined the light along the edge of the floor and up and down the side of the bookcase. "It's gone." He switched off the flashlight and turned.

Holly wasn't looking at him or at the floor or the

bookcase. Her head was angled toward the sofa, and she looked extremely pale. "Holly," said Landon, "what?" He twisted to look, too. The pages in the Bible were turning.

Suddenly Holly stepped toward Landon and took hold of his arm. Hard.

Landon hardly noticed the squeeze. He felt amazed but also secretly pleased. "That's like before," he said softly. "Just like last time. . .except then the Bible was on the desk." He made a halfhearted motion behind him. "And there had been a breeze in the room."

The air was still as could be. Not even a gentle draft. This made the movement of the pages even eerier. They were truly turning on their own. Unless there was someone or something else turning them.

The pages stopped. Landon was about to take a step toward the Bible when Holly clutched tighter and held him back. She felt as stiff as a statue. "Holly," said Landon in a soothing tone. "You can let go. It's the Bible. I want to take a look."

It lay open to Genesis, the first book of the Bible. Automatically, Landon scanned the page for underlining. At first he didn't see it. Then he realized his own shadow was covering the page. He moved to the side to unblock the ceiling light's glow. There they were—a series of neat lines running beneath the first six verses of Genesis, chapter 3. Landon read aloud, though in a hushed voice: " 'Now the serpent was more subtil than any beast of the field which the Lord God had made. And he said unto the woman, Yea, hath God said, Ye shall not eat of every tree of the garden?

" 'And the woman said unto the serpent, We may eat of the fruit of the trees of the garden: But of the fruit of the tree which is in the midst of the garden, God hath said, Ye shall not eat of it, neither shall ye touch it, lest ye die.

" 'And the serpent said unto the woman, Ye shall not surely die: For God doth know that in the day ye eat thereof, then your eyes shall be opened, and ye shall be as gods, knowing good and evil.

" 'And when the woman saw that the tree was good for food, and that it was pleasant to the eyes, and a tree to be desired to make one wise, she took of the fruit thereof, and did eat, and gave also unto her husband with her; and he did eat.' "

As soon as Landon said "eat," the pages began flipping. It felt strange indeed to be holding a book as its pages rattled and turned on their own. At one point the Bible gave a tug, as if someone were trying to yank it away and throw it on the sofa. Landon held on.

When the pages stopped, Landon quickly found the underlining. It was in the Gospel of Matthew, chapter 4, verse 16. With Holly peeking over his shoulder, again Landon read in a soft, reverent tone: " 'The people which sat in darkness saw great light; and to them which sat in the region and shadow of death light is sprung up.' "

The pages turned and soon stopped at a page where Landon found these words underlined in John 3:19–21: " 'And this is the condemnation, that light is come into the world, and men loved darkness rather than light, because their deeds were evil. For every one that doeth evil hateth the light, neither cometh to the light, lest his deeds should be reproved. But he that doeth truth cometh to the light, lest his deeds may be made manifest, that they are wrought in God.' "

A few pages flipped all at once. Slightly trembling (or was

it Holly shaking against him?), Landon read the marked words from John 12:35–36: " 'Then Jesus said unto them, Yet a little while is the light with you. Walk while ye have the light, lest darkness come upon you: for he that walketh in darkness knoweth not whither he goeth. While ye have light, believe in the light, that ye may be the children of the light. These things spake Jesus, and departed, and did hide himself from them.' "

Landon waited, but the Bible remained still save for the quivering from his arms. Leaving it open to that page, Landon carefully set the heavy, old book down. He wanted to ask Holly if she believed him now. But he couldn't get himself to do it. Instead, he merely waited to see what she might say.

After what seemed an eternity of listening to his sister's light, shallow breathing, Landon finally heard her say, "Did you understand any of that? It sounded like Shakespeare or another language or something."

Landon had grown somewhat accustomed to the King James style. He'd been reading it occasionally since receiving the old Bible for his eleventh birthday in October. "Well," he said in only a slightly superior tone, "it is a bit archaic sounding to untrained ears, I suppose." He wasn't sure where he'd heard that expression—"untrained ears"—before, but he felt pretty smart saying it.

Holly jabbed him with her elbow. "Just tell me what it said. Does it mean something? I was. . .uh. . .I was just a little scared to really listen. That's all."

Landon took a deep breath, swelling his chest as if he hadn't been afraid in the least. Keeping one eye on the Bible, Landon tried to sneak a peek at the bookcase and the floor. It was a lot easier pretending he wasn't scared when there were no moving book parts and creeping shadows to contend with. Confident that things were normal, at least for the moment, Landon thought about what he'd read, and he tried to explain.

"Well, the first part was about Adam and Eve in the garden, and the snake—"

"The serpent," said Holly.

"I thought you weren't listening," Landon chided.

"I hate snakes. And serpents. And all things slithery." Holly shuddered. "Unfortunately, I did hear that part."

"So you heard that the serpent"—Landon stuck out his tongue—"got Eve to eat the fruit she wasn't supposed to. That God had said 'Don't' for that tree."

"And then Adam ate, too," Holly added.

"Right. And that's when the pages flipped to the New Testament, to Matthew and John, but I don't remember the verse numbers now. There was something about darkness and light and evil—"

"And a shadow of death," Holly said with a lingering lisp.

"Yeah," said Landon. "A shadow." He took a deep breath, bent over the open Bible, held his hand over the page, and then touched the ancient, thin paper. "Maybe I can find the other words again. . ."

But he'd hardly begun riffling the pages when he felt Holly tugging on his arm. "Landon," she said softly.

"Hold on, Holly. Let me see—"

"Knowledge of good and evil, darkness and light, and a shadow." Something in her voice caused Landon to pause. The hairs on the back of his neck were rising.

"Holly," he said more sharply than he meant to, "let go of my arm. Just let me find these—"

"A shadow!" Holly whispered tensely as her grip fell from Landon's elbow.

Somehow Landon knew what was happening before he saw it. When he turned his head, his suspicion was confirmed. The tall bookcase was gliding gradually and quietly away from the wall, swinging around like an invitation to a crypt.

"Are we dreaming?" Holly said breathily. "Are you in my dream, Landon? Or am I in yours?"

"We're in the same dream," said Landon. "Except that it's real."

Chapter Three

There was a look in Holly's eyes that Landon had never seen before.

"The dream-stone," she said. "When we went to the library on your birthday and Grandpa Karl's hands were all bandaged. . .you ran in first. I watched you. You ran past Bart's grave and went into his first cabin, the reading room that no one ever goes into. When you went in, you didn't have your stone." Holly shook her head. "But when you came out"—she started to nod—"you were holding it like it was your birthday present."

"It was my birthday present," said Landon. He held up the Bible. "And so was this."

"I know," said Holly, "but it was bugging me forever how you did that. I mean, how the stone got in there ahead of you. It was weird. And then you finally tell me the story today—"

"Which you didn't believe."

"Well, I know, but now this!" Holly pointed at the dark

doorway. "This is weird, but I believe you. So this goes to the library, right?"

A musty odor wafted into the room. At the base of the opening, mist plumed like dry ice flowing and curling on a stage.

"Last I checked," said Landon. "Down and underground and then up again, right into Bart's log cabin reading room."

"Well," said Holly, "you up for it? I mean, we're in this together now, and I did say I was ready for some adventuring."

Landon felt a chill penetrating the air from the passageway. It was February. He looked at Holly's jacket, hat—which was still on her head—and mittens tucked into her pocket. His clothes were still on, so he just needed his own jacket and gloves. Once he had them on, he picked up the flashlight, wrapped the loop around his wrist, and reluctantly left the Bible resting open atop the sleeping bag. "I left the dream-stone at home," he said, half-wishing this would discourage Holly from their midnight escapade. But she merely shrugged her shoulders and said, "Oh, well." So Landon shrugged, too, and then he sighed, and then after checking to make sure the bedroom door was secure, he flipped on the flashlight and turned out the ceiling light. Holly gasped.

"You're sure you're up for this?" Landon said teasingly, trying to cover his own nervousness.

"Of. . .of course. If you are."

Landon stepped to the doorway and shone the beam down the stairs. Ah yes, it was all coming back to him. The stone steps went straight down until he could hardly make them out, though they appeared to turn to the left.

"We should have brought two flashlights," he said, really thinking if he'd left the one in his hand at home, they probably wouldn't be doing this. Why was it that he was more anxious about going down these steps and into the tunnel this time than the first? Perhaps because then he had been driven by sheer curiosity and excitement. And he'd been naive as to how much darkness lay before him. Now he knew about the darkness and about the potential dead end at the top of the stairs at the far end of the tunnel.

"Stay close," said Landon, but Holly was already pressing in behind him. "But don't push," Landon said. "These stairs are steep."

"Okay," said Holly, practically breathing into his ear. "Let's go."

"To the BUL!" said Landon.

He had to admit it. Walking down the long, dark, damp tunnel with his sister breathing down his neck was a tad more pleasant than going it alone. And there was some comfort in knowing that should they be trapped at the top of the stairs at the end of the tunnel, he wouldn't be forced to talk to himself to keep from going mad. He could talk to Holly, and they could drive each other crazy as his flashlight batteries wore down.

Between such thoughts, Landon was aware of Holly tapping him continuously on the shoulder, right in rhythm with their walking.

"Why are you doing that?" Landon said before ducking beneath a stalactite of dirt.

"A hundred seventy-four, a hundred seventy-five. . ."

Landon stopped, and so did Holly's tapping. "You're counting?" he said turning but keeping the light shining forward. "What on earth for?"

"For pacing," said Holly. She kept repeating the last number quietly as they stood in place. "Besides," she added, "we're under the earth, not on it. A hundred seventy-five, a hundred seventy-five. . ."

"What? Oh. We're on it and under it. Never mind." Landon resumed his march amid the rocky walls and ceiling.

"A hundred seventy-six," came Holly's voice from behind. Then she fell quiet except for her soft tapping on his shoulder. Landon had to shake his head to quit counting paces himself. The numbers were ticking through his brain against his will.

By the time they reached the stairs, Landon's ears were nearly numb from cold. He held the flashlight between his legs and cupped his ears, but it didn't help. The outsides of his gloves were cold as well. He breathed into his palms and tried again, hurrying to carry some warmth to his ears. He could hear a sound like the ocean and then the rasp of his own breathing. It was time to climb the stairs.

"Hey," said Holly. "Look. Glass."

Sure enough. Tiny bits of glass sparkled under the flashlight's beam. The fragments appeared fairly well embedded and ground into the floor, almost as if they had been trampled on. Or perhaps, Landon thought, the lens had truly shattered into a million pieces.

He swung the beam toward the corner and saw a ribbed cylinder of steel.

"Grandpa's flashlight!" Holly exclaimed, and Landon flicked the beam over her face so he could catch her expression. She blinked in the light, but Landon could tell her eyes had been wide in astonishment. "I really believe you now, Landon. I mean, I think I might believe just about everything you've ever said!"

Landon laughed. "Except that I was listening to Ms. Gillersby in class."

"What? Oh, that. Well, everybody lies to their teachers."

Landon grinned but shined the light away so Holly couldn't see him.

"Now to count the steps," Holly said, seemingly to herself.

"So how many paces was the tunnel?" asked Landon.

"I've got it," said Holly. "I won't forget."

"You're not going to tell me?"

"Shh. Let's go. Three, four. . ."

Landon was tempted to call out random numbers to confuse her, but he refrained. She was his sister, after all. And she was going on an adventure with him. Most of all, she believed his story, and he could probably get away with saying anything at all to her from now on. That was certainly worth something. So he let her count the steps in peace.

The way was blocked at the top of the stairway, as expected. Landon used his flashlight to tap the solid wood wall rimmed by rock. "Bookcase," he said leaning against it. He didn't put his full weight into it because it wouldn't budge. He sighed. "Last time, after I'd pretty much given up on ever getting through here, I went back down the steps and said what I'd read in the Bible earlier that night. 'Visions and dreams,' I said. That's what opened this bookcase, I think, and the other one."

"Grandpa Karl's?"

"Yeah."

"Well, how did Grandpa's open tonight?"

Landon felt stunned. Oh, no! He couldn't believe he hadn't paid better attention to what was said in his grandfather's study. Then again, he didn't know exactly when the bookcase had begun to swing open. "One of us said something that triggered it," he said. "But what did you say?"

"I just asked what you had said when you read the Shakespeare stuff."

"It's not Shakespeare," said Landon. "It's the Bible."

"I know," she said, "but it has all those dith's and doth's and doeth's and stuff."

Landon tried to think. With a sinking heart, he realized that he had read all the Bible passages aloud, and there was no way he would remember any precise phrases or verses. "I should have brought it along. Then I could just read it out loud again."

Holly sighed with exasperation. "You mean you really don't know how to open this? And we're stuck here. . .underground?"

"We're not underground, anymore. I think we're inside the outer wall. Just let me think for a second." He rested his elbows against the wood and pressed his knuckles to either side of his head.

"How did you do it last time, again?" said Holly, a tinge of panic in her voice.

"I was going back down the steps, and I think I said, 'visions and dreams.' " Landon waited, hoping maybe this phrase would work again. It didn't. With a rising sense of panic, his mind began to race. What if he and Holly shouted words, any words, in any order—might they happen upon the correct key that would open the bookcase? It was like trying to guess at the password to a computer system. No, Landon thought, it had to be something that had been said in Grandpa Karl's study. He closed his eyes to concentrate. He'd been reading from his Bible. . .about what?

"Adam and Eve," he said aloud. "Garden of Eden. Uh. . . serpent!"

Holly jumped. "Where?"

"No," said Landon. "I'm trying to figure out what we said that got Grandpa Karl's bookcase to open."

"You mean when God told them not to go to the tree, and the serpent said, 'Ye surely shall not dieth, but ye will knoweth all good and evil'? Or something like that."

Landon sensed a slight movement of air. "Did you feel that?" he asked.

"I did feel something, or thought I saw something, but it's so dark. It was like the darkness itself was moving. Landon, this is getting creepy."

"Good and evil," Landon said. It happened again as if the rock walls had turned into a thousand big black spiders and then shifted back to rock again. Yet Landon knew the rock hadn't changed. " 'It was like the darkness itself was moving,' " he said, thinking out loud. "Holly, I think that's it. The first part I read was about good and evil." The blackness shifted around them, and Holly gasped. "The second part was about"—he paused and touched the wood wall—"darkness and light."

The wall moved away, and he kept pressing it as if he had pushed it open.

"It worked," said Holly excitedly. She was holding
Landon by his jacket, and she pushed him from the stone step
into Bart's reading room. She breathed deeply. "It was getting
a little claustrophobic in there. And those rocks or whatever
that was. . .*ugh*." She shivered.

They stepped into the room, which was Bartholomew's
original log cabin from a very long time ago. Landon shone
the flashlight. A rugged wood chair stood in the center facing
the fireplace to the right. Three logs sat in the fireplace,
unburned, as they had for years. Over the mantel was mounted
a very large fish, its mouth open and its tail curved up.

"It looks so different at night," said Holly.

"Everything does," Landon said knowingly. "At least this
time I've got a flashlight. Last time—"

"I know, I know. Tumble and crash. How did you do it all
alone in the dark? I would have screamed my head off."

Landon didn't answer. The more impressed his sister
seemed with him, the more puffed up he felt. It felt good.
He'd let his calm silence speak for itself.

Even though he had retrieved it the very next day, he
had to go over to the far wall and scan the floor where his
dream-stone had come to rest after he'd hurled it up from
the stairway. "This is where I found it, Holly, when I ran
ahead—Holly?"

Landon turned around. She wasn't in the room. With a
sigh, he headed for the doorway to the library's foyer, but as
he reached it, something made him pause and look toward
the open bookcase. There is no other way to describe what
he saw than that it looked like darkness was leaking from
the black chasm and silently trickling along the edge of the

floor. As Landon moved the flashlight, the gliding line of blackness seemed to stay just ahead of the beam. It turned the corner and started in his direction. For a moment Landon felt rooted to the floor. At the last instant, he hopped over the threshold to the marble floor of the foyer, his shoes making a soft smacking sound. Moving away from the reading room, Landon directed the light across the wide space. "Holly?" he tried again.

The light caught the outline of Bart's tombstone, the front end of a rowboat with an oar sticking out on either side. Jutting up from the prow was the shape of an open book. Of course neither the boat nor the book was "real"; they were carved from stone.

A head popped up from behind the book, and Landon caught his breath.

"Over here," said Holly. "You said this is where you read the first part of the Auctor's Riddle, right? Well, come and look at this."

Forgetting about the strange, snakelike shadow, Landon hurried to join his sister. In the glow of the flashlight, the gold inlaid letters appeared to jump right from the black stone page:

The seeker of knowledge is often torn
From the day one dies to the day one is born
Over what to embrace and what to scorn
Some leads to grace; others leave forlorn.

"Do you understand any of that?" asked Holly.
Landon could see his sister's frown. "It sounds like Vates,"

he said, his heart beating with excitement. "He writes strange stuff like this."

"It sounds so serious. What do you think it means? You're the word lover in the family."

Landon blushed a little. This message wasn't a riddle with question marks, but it seemed just as puzzling. "I guess it means to be careful what you want to know." He knew he didn't sound too confident.

"Hunh," said Holly matter-of-factly. "I thought all knowledge was good. The more you know the better."

"I don't know," said Landon. Then he remembered something. "After I'd read the Auctor's Riddle here, I went into the library and—"

"We're in the library, Landon."

He sighed. "I went into the collection room and—"

"You climbed the *Book of Meanings*, I know. Should we do that? Do you think it will grow again?"

The thought of the climb didn't exactly thrill Landon. It had been a long, arduous climb by the end of which he'd been feeling rather loopy and exhausted. He didn't like feeling that way and would prefer not to have to experience it again. But how else would he get back to Wonderwood to see Vates and Melech and Ditty and Hardy? Could there be another way without going through the *Book of Meanings*?

"I don't know," said Landon answering Holly's questions as well as his own. "Maybe we could ask the other books about it. Come on!" He waved the flashlight, and for a split second, the great chandelier high overhead sparkled like a bursting firework. Landon led the way to the hallway that lay between the foyer and the main collection room. As he and

Holly passed between the portraits of Button Up's forefathers and ancient dignitaries, Landon suddenly clicked off the light. He also slowed down, and Holly bumped right into him.

"Why'd you do that?" she said in a whisper.

"I don't want to startle them or scare them off," said Landon.

"Who?" asked Holly, gazing back and forth among the portraits.

"The books," Landon said. "Now *shh*."

He crept to the corner and peeked into the vast room, waiting for his eyes to adjust to the darkness and the great space before him.

Windows ran high up around the perimeter of the room, allowing in faint light from the faraway stars. The towering walls of books created a fortress. *A fortress of knowledge and adventure,* thought Landon. He knew what awaited them in the very center of the room: the voluminous *Book of Meanings.* Its wooden stand had been replaced with a more solid and decorative one than before, Grandpa Karl had reported earlier. No one but Landon—and now Holly—knew the reason the other one had been discovered beneath the book and around it on the floor in a flattened spread of splinters. Somehow the *Book of Meanings* itself had shrunk back to its normal—albeit quite large—size. And everything else in the library had returned to its previous state—even the epitaph on Bart's tombstone.

That is, until tonight.

Beyond the reference section that contained the wondrous *Book of Meanings* rose the twisting stairway and shooting catwalks of "the tree." The black metal framework provided access to every level of books along the walls. And for those unafraid of heights, the top walkways also offered delightful aerial views of the room. After climbing the *Book of Meanings* when it was as high as a mountain and falling from the sky on the back of his horse friend, Melech, Landon didn't consider himself very fearful of heights.

The library was totally silent.

"This way," whispered Landon over his shoulder, and he proceeded stealthily into the room, heading to his left. When Landon reached the corner of the speaking books, he scanned their spines anxiously. Motioning Holly over, he said, "Right here." As he pointed at the books, Holly looked at Landon and raised her eyebrows. As much as Landon hoped for a book to speak, he was also tense with anxiety. It was like watching as someone drew a needle toward a taut balloon, waiting for it to—

"Young man?"

The voice caused Landon and Holly to jump. Landon glanced quickly at Holly, hoping she hadn't noticed him flinch.

"Yes!" said Landon, scanning the books. "Hello! Remember me?"

"How could we forget? You were the bearer of bad tidings. And the climber of the *Book of Meanings*. No, no, young man. We shan't ever forget you, I'm afraid."

Other voices murmured things like "There he is!" and "It's him again!" and "Hold on to your covers, books; looks like we're in for another crazy night!"

"Bad tidings?" said Landon. "What bad tidings?"

"Oh, it's not feally your rault," said a familiar and sheepish voice near the lower corner. It was the dyslexic book.

"Mean I, the nad bews was that our owner was dead. We just, well, we knadn't hown before you old tus. At's thall."

"No, that's not all. That's not all at all, I'm afraid!"

Landon thought it was *Platitudes*. That book seemed the most talkative of the bunch.

"As if the sad, bad, and most disheartening of newses weren't enough, the boy here had to go and"—it made a sniffling, scoffing sort of noise—"and desecrate the revered *Book of Meanings*! How dare he deposit himself between its most illustrious pages! And then force them to bring in. . . that thing. That hideous monster of a noise-making machine. That. . .that vacuum cleaner."

A number of books shuddered on the shelves while making gasping, sucking noises.

"Oh, come off it, Platty!" said a voice from high up and to the right. "It wasn't all the boy's fault. He merely did what he had to do. You told him to go look in the book."

Landon heard some murmurs of assent and felt a little better. He hadn't been expecting such an unwelcome welcome.

"Well, all that aside," said Platitudes, "things did change around here after that night—and not for the better, I might add."

The books grumbled and seemed to be agreeing with this, as well.

"What changed?" asked Landon. "What happened?"

"I'll tell him," said a low, husky voice Landon didn't remember hearing before. It came from the second shelf off the floor near his right shin. "I'm a geometry book, by the way, who has been stuck over here for a decade with these yahoos. My name's *Fun with Lines, Planes, and Cubes*, and I'm in the wrong section. Obviously. Anyway, complaining aside, I see what goes on from a slightly different angle than the rest, if you catch my meaning."

Landon crouched down so he was nearer the book. Though he could sense the other books were listening, he spoke quietly as if only for the geometry book's ears.

"Well, what did you see?" said Landon curiously.

"I'll tell you what I saw. While *Platitudes*, *Attitudes*, and the rest of these ninnies who love to hear the squawks of their own voices were being so mesmerized by your shenanigans climbing their beloved *Book of Meanings*, I was keeping a lookout, see, on what the cat dragged in."

"The cat?" said Landon.

"That's you, boy, and that night you were wearing the cat's pajamas as I recall. A nice blue-and-white striped number. Yeah, you remember."

Landon did remember wearing his pajamas and being barefoot, but he didn't understand what this book was talking about.

"All right, all right. I'll quit talking in circumferences and give it to you straight. Point A to point B. While you were off gallivanting up the big book, I was watching your six and tracing your trail back to your point of origin. That is—you came in from the hallway, point A, moved to just about where you're standing now, point B, and then turned and headed straightaway for Mr. Big Book, point C. I calculated it as precisely a forty-three-degree angle."

"You're getting off on a tangent, Geo-germ!"

A number of voices laughed.

"Your father was a pamphlet!" the geometry book retorted. It lowered its voice. "Sorry, kid. I hate it over here. Now where was I?"

"A forty-three-degree angle."

"Oh, yeah. Well, the thing of it was, as you ascended Ω Mightiness of Meanings over there, I was estimating the escalating trajectories from point A to your position on the book. Let's call your position point Y. So I was going back and forth as you were going up and up. A to Y, A to Y, the ever-increasing arc of altitude. And that's when I noticed them."

"Them?" said Landon. "What are you talking about?"

"The shadows coming in from point A. First a small trickle and then a steady stream of darkness. A leak from the underground is the only way I can explain it. These shadows slithered in like silent snakes, sneaking across the floor and sliding up the shelves and slipping in among the books. Made everyone pretty squeamish, see? And we still don't know what they're up to, though it can't be any good."

The book of geometry paused, and Landon sensed restlessness among the other volumes. It seemed they were all looking for snaky shadows. Landon swallowed a lump of guilt as he thought of the strange line he'd seen squiggle in behind him from the stone stairwell behind the bookcase. A leak from the underground? He swallowed again, feeling a growing lump of fear.

"Say," said the low, husky voice, "who's the blond?"

Landon turned his head, looked up, and stood. "Holly! You scared me. I forgot you were here. I'm sorry. Were you right behind me this whole time? Holly?"

Holly was clasping her knit cap before her chest, gently

wringing it back and forth as she gazed at the rows of books. Finally, she spoke in a faint little voice. "They talk, Landon. And you're talking with them. To books."

"Oh, brother," said a voice. "Not this routine again."

"No, no," said another voice. "I believe it's 'oh, sister' this time."

"Yes," said Landon, pulling her up alongside him. "This is my sister Holly. Holly, um, these are the books I was telling you about."

She released her cap with one hand and gave a little wave. "Hi," she said.

A chorus of "Hi" and "Hello" and "How do you do?" rang out. Then the low, husky voice said, "They're coming in again, kid. Look behind you. The shadows. . ."

Landon forced himself to look. At first he couldn't see anything unusual. There were all sorts of normal shadows stretched here and there throughout the room. But then Landon saw it. Or rather, them. The floor itself seemed to be turning into a sea of living, writhing, black serpents, except they didn't have bodies, and they made absolutely no sound. Yet their rippling and squiggling motion was enough to make Landon nearly sick with dread.

Before this moving mass reached their corner, Landon grabbed Holly's arm and yanked her toward the nearest reading table. Stepping onto a chair and then up onto the table, Landon hoisted Holly up after him and held her close. He couldn't tell if the trembling was coming from her or from him or both.

As the silent swarm slithered past, the geometry book called out in a voice that was sounding less low and husky by the moment, "Oh, no. I've never seen so many! What will they do to us?"

Landon was finding it hard to think, let alone speak. From deep in his throat, he dug out his voice, and though there was no need for loudness, he found himself fairly shouting, "How can we stop them? What are they?"

"To the first question—I don't know. To the second, we have come up with a name."

The shadows were spreading, climbing the walls of books like rising waves. Afraid the surge of darkness would suddenly come crashing down on them, Landon could hardly bear to keep his eyes open. What would it be like to be engulfed by these silent waves of shadows?

When it seemed they could reach no farther and no higher, they disappeared. The darkness was absorbed by the bookshelves like oil sinking into a sponge.

Landon trembled. Even his jaw quivered uncontrollably.

"Wh–wh–what do you c–c–call them?" said Landon.

"Bookwyrmen," said a voice, pronouncing it the German way, "Book-*vermin*."

Landon was mouthing this strange name to himself when an eerie noise made him cringe. Hundreds of books were choking and gasping as if they were being strangled.

Chapter Four

Landon and Holly stood a long time on the reading table, the only sounds in the library coming from their knees knocking and their feet jiggling against the smooth wood surface. It sounded like they were doing a little soft shoe number. The truth, of course, was that their "dancing on the table" had nothing to do with being silly or happy and everything to do with being worried and scared.

"You. . .you. . .you. . . ," Holly said through her chattering teeth.

A minute later she said, "You. . .you. . .you didn't tell me about that. About them. About the sh–sh–shadows!"

"I didn't know," said Landon weakly. He still felt guilty and fearful for having let in the bookwyrmen. But was it really his fault? Where did they come from? "The underground," the geometry book had said. Landon remembered seeing one snaky shadow back in Grandpa Karl's study. It had slipped behind the bookcase, which did lead to the stone stairway that did lead to the tunnel underground. And the creeping shadow he'd seen come into Bart's reading room also came from that passage. Still, something seemed to tell Landon that it wasn't so simple as that. He'd gone through that tunnel twice, and he shuddered to think about ever going down there again.

"Really, Holly, I don't know where they came from. I don't think it's just the tunnel. I don't know."

Despite it being the middle of the night, eventually the library regained a sense of normalcy about it. Whatever had happened was done. Everything was quiet. Pretty soon Landon and Holly looked at each other. They felt a little funny about hugging each other atop the table.

"Do you think it's safe to get down now?" asked Holly.

Landon released his clutch on her and took a half step back. "Yeah," he said, nodding and then looking down, "I do. Uh, ladies first." He made a sweeping gesture with his hand and noticed the flashlight dangling from his wrist. He glanced at the swinging plastic tube and then at Holly.

"Uh, how about age before beauty?" She dipped her head and began swishing her hand in a circle.

Landon smirked. "Fine. It's no problem. What could little shadows do to us, anyway? They're probably harmless, right?"

Holly's swishing hand froze. She frowned, squinting toward the floor. "Landon?"

"Yes?"

"There's still one out there on the floor."

Landon slowly turned and scanned the area where his sister was looking. He traced a visual path along the baseboard. From point A to point. . .

Landon paused, straining his eyes. He went back slowly. . .there.

"Why, you little bugger," Landon muttered. Keeping his eyes trained on the smudgy strip (which is hard to do without blinking or looking away, especially in very dim light), he eased his flashlight arm down until the plastic tube rested against his palm. Gripping the flashlight and finding the switch with his thumb, Landon slowly brought it up as if he were silently unsheathing a sword. When he had it aimed at the shadow, he flipped the switch. "Ha!"

The shadow snake zipped over and up and disappeared between two books, one of which looked like *Fun with Lines, Planes, and Cubes*.

"That thing was fast," said Landon, his heart pounding with excitement. Now that the light was on, he waved it back and forth along the floor and up and down among the shelves. Of course the beam caused other shadows to appear and move from the shifting light. But these were normal shadows, not snake shadows that seemed to have a mind of their own.

After sweeping the floor with the flashlight around the table several times to be sure it was clear (the shadows from chairs and table legs had Landon doing double takes), with wobbly knees, Landon finally hopped down, and Holly followed.

"Why don't you turn off that light?" said a book, or at least a voice from one of the shelves.

Landon didn't recognize the voice. He turned and swung the flashlight beam across the books. Tiny squelching, squeaking sounds came out, almost as if the books were in pain.

"Please!" pleaded the voice. "We've suffered enough for one night. Turn out that light!"

Confused, Landon obeyed. As soon as the light was extinguished, the voice from the shelf let out a sigh of relief that sounded like a hiss. "Thanksss. That'sss better."

The books remained mysteriously quiet. Landon thought he detected movement somewhere, something he couldn't quite see or really hear. He was tempted to pull out a book and quickly shine his light into the gap to see if anything was going on. But he was also nervous. He wasn't sure he really wanted to see what was back there.

"*Platitudes*? *Attitudes*? Uh, *Latitudes*," Landon called toward the lower corner where the dyslexic book was shelved, "or whatever your title is, anyone still here?"

A voice cleared its throat. "A-hmm. Hey, bud. Kid. You know—you. And you, too, sister. Come on over here."

It sounded like the geometry book and seemed to come from that location, yet somehow it didn't sound like the same personality as before. Landon looked at Holly. She shrugged, and he shrugged back. They stepped closer to the shelf and crouched down. "Yeah," said Landon being careful not to lean too near. If any sort of shadow were to touch his body, he would probably scream.

"I'm not just a geometry book, you know."

Landon waited.

Holly asked, "What do you mean?"

"I mean," said the voice, "that I contain mathematical information that no one in the world has yet obtained. Not even any computer."

A gasp of astonishment slipped from Holly's lips.

"Mathematical information? Like, like numbers?"

"Oh, for badness' sake, yes. Numbers like you wouldn't believe and then some. I'm talking charts of the numbers of the stars—all the stars in the universe—seen and unseen by man. I'm talking numbers of fish in all known waterways—and all unknown-to-man sea passages. I'm talking totals for each species, sum totals, food-chain totals, depth-level figures multiplied exponentially by water pressure per cubic inch."

Landon had no idea what it was talking about, but Holly appeared to be fairly drooling.

"Wait a second," said Landon shaking his head. "How is that even possible?"

"Wha–a–a–t?" said the voice, dropping its tone sarcastically. "Food-chain totals? Well, it's simple, really. You begin at the bottom of the marine food chain and work your way up. The tinier the species, the greater its numbers. So for every one killer whale, for instance—"

"What?" Landon frowned. His head was starting to hurt. "Wait. No. I mean, how is it possible to count all the stars—even the ones you can't see? That doesn't make sense. No one could do that. And someone had to record those numbers in"—he reached toward the geometry book but then withdrew his hand—"well, in you."

"Tssk, tssk, tssk," said the voice. "Thiss iss mosst dissappointing." It sighed. "Well if you don't care to know how many grains of sand fill Death Valley, or how many atoms make up your body, or—"

"I care," said Holly eagerly. "I'd like to know those numbers. What pages are they on?"

She was reaching for the book when the voice said, "Stop.

You don't think it'ss sso ssimple as that now, do you?"

"Well," said Holly, "I thought—"

"No. Now listen to me. You know I'm in the wrong ssection, right? Here'ss what I want you to do. Take me from the shelf—go ahead."

Holly grasped the leather binding. Landon held his breath as he watched her slide the volume out.

"That's it. Now if you'll kindly carry me to the tree over there. . ."

"The tree?" said Holly standing with the book. "Oh, the stairway over there."

"Yess, yess," said the book. "The tree."

As Holly walked away, Landon's tongue stuck to the roof of his mouth. Something seemed terribly wrong, but he couldn't put his finger on it. He wasn't familiar with every section of the library, but he'd studied the layout well enough to know that the math books were located on the wall opposite from where he stood. Why was the book telling Holly to go to the tree?

He stood to follow her, feeling both concerned and curious. As he took a step, he thought he heard something behind him. Was one of the other books finally speaking up? Perhaps *Platitudes* would have something helpful to say. Looking back at the books and waiting, Landon finally sighed. They were silent. But something told him they didn't want to be silent. It was as if they were waiting. Or—Landon didn't want to think this, but it came to him anyway—or the books were being muffled or gagged against their will.

All right, Landon told himself. *Now you're just thinking crazy.* Books being gagged! He'd better catch up to Holly.

She was carrying the book before her as if it were a precious relic, marching around the reference section and on toward the tree.

Landon paused beside a case of encyclopedias to gaze at the *Book of Meanings*. "So you're not going to grow tonight," he said in a soft, reverent tone. "Or are you?"

Taking a deep breath, Landon planted one foot deliberately in front of him. Nothing happened. He took another step, and then another toward the tome, but it sat unchanged atop its ornate stand. Finally, Landon walked right up to it, rose to his tiptoes, and peered into the book. A strange sensation swept through him as he dragged his fingertip up the edges of the pages and across to the top right corner.

"It's so easy now," he said lifting the thin sheaf of paper. He brought it up and over, flinching slightly as he remembered last October when he had hung on for dear life before dropping to the other side.

"Well," he said, "I guess I don't get to go through you again." Landon grasped each side of the stand as if he were about to deliver a speech or sermon. "No, I don't think I'd fit. Not that you're not big. You are. But not like last time."

After taking another deep breath and heaving a sigh, Landon stepped back from the stand and turned. He looked at the floor and shuffled his feet, swinging the flashlight from his wrist. He wasn't sad about not being able to climb the book, but the truth was he would gladly go through those adventures again if it meant he could see his friends.

"Melech," Landon said just to hear the sound of the horse's name. "Ditty, Hardy, Vates." He laughed and looked up. He had started to waggle his head and was about to say "Ho, Ludo!" when he realized his sister was nowhere in sight.

"Holly? Where are you?"

Landon flicked on the flashlight and raised it. The girderlike limbs of the tree appeared ominously overhead, reaching in every direction. Fat line shadows appeared high on the ceiling, moving this way and that. The catwalks seemed to multiply with shadows, creating an unending geometrical pattern leading upward.

"That stupid geometry book—in the wrong section. Nobody knows how many stars there are." Landon scoffed. He sure wished Holly would show up. Where had the book taken her, anyway? Or rather, where had she taken the book?

Landon reached the base of the twisting trunk of stairs. After shining the flashlight beam around the library and saying his sister's name three more times, he climbed one step and stopped, realizing something. The floor had made a tinny sound when he'd stepped from it to the metal stairway of the tree. The tree was metal, but it was so thick and sturdy that it barely rang at all under people's footsteps. As Landon paused and listened, he noticed something else. The gentlest of drafts was coming up from below him, accompanied by a faint and hollow echo.

Landon looked down and shone the flashlight. Rather than seeing carpeted floor, he observed a metal grate that reminded him of a sewer cover in a street. Wait—something had been painted across the surface of the metal grid. White stenciled letters read: KEEP OUT. Landon stooped over. Beneath the grate, a series of steps wound down into the ground. With a sinking feeling, he wondered if that was where Holly had gone. *Not underground again,* he thought miserably. *Oh, no.*

"She's gone down, I'm afraid, kid. Nothing I could do."

Landon jumped at the voice, flailing the flashlight around. The beam passed over a book propped up by its covers in the shape of an A on the floor nearby. It was the geometry book.

"You!" said Landon with rising rage. "What have you done to her? Where has she gone? And. . ." He paused and tried to collect his thoughts. "Why are you out here?"

"It wasn't me! That's what I'm saying! Those dastardly bookwyrmen talked her right into it. Oh," it added in anguish, "I feel so—so used."

"The bookwyrmen?" said Landon skeptically. "Those shadow snakes? How could they make her go down there? What happened?"

"Hey, I'm just two covers and a binding around pages with ink on them. A dark shadow comes in, covers my words, and fills in the spaces with whatever words it wants. Makes me say things I never intended to say. Or keeps me from saying anything at all."

"They can do that? Make you say things that aren't true?"

"That's all they do is make us books tell lies. Yes, I'm afraid they can do this to us. But with you, kid, no. They can't make you do anything—"

"But my sister. You. . .they—"

"Didn't make her do anything. It was all a trick to get her interested, curious, and confused. You should have heard the things they promised her! I was trying to scream out and warn her, but she couldn't hear me. Once a bookwyrm begins to tickle your ear, it's hard for you to listen to anything else."

"What did they promise her?"

"They promised her knowledge of—well—everything."

"Everything?"

"Everything, including dark and secret things no man, woman, or child should ever know about."

A flicker of curiosity arose in Landon's heart. "What kinds of 'dark and secret things'?"

"Don't you see?" cried the book. "That's just how she got into trouble! Though they can't make you do anything at the start, once you've agreed to do what they say, you've given them some of your power. Then they can use that power against you and against others. And they will."

Every second they spent talking was another second Holly was getting farther away. Landon was about to set down the flashlight, when the grate suddenly seemed to wisp like smoke. Instead of saying KEEP OUT, it said COME IN. Landon blinked. When he looked again, it was back to saying KEEP OUT. He tapped the grate with the flashlight. After one hard *click*, it fell right through, and Landon almost tumbled into the hole.

"Whoa!" Landon rocked back on his heels. The grate had turned to shadowy smoke. The words COME IN swirled in the center, and Landon thought he heard a soft voice whispering them, too. "Come in. . .come in!"

Landon plunged his leg through the smoke and began to climb down.

"Don't listen to it—to them!" The book urged. "They're shape shifters and form drifters! The bookwyrmen are shadows that cannot be trusted. Don't listen to them; that's how your sister got into trouble!"

Landon had stepped down, and now he looked up. The grate looked solid again, and when he tapped it, a metallic clinking echoed down the winding stairs.

Chapter Five

Beads of sweat broke out on Landon's forehead, and his skin prickled as if touched by a thousand needles. He was running down the stairs. He wanted to get away from the shadows up above. He also wanted to find Holly and rescue her from whatever had enticed her to come below. But how would they get out? What if the grate remained solid? They would be trapped down there forever.

Such morbid thoughts didn't help, so he tried to push them aside.

He was huffing as his legs churned down the steps. Round and round he went like a drill bit driving into the earth. How deep did it go? Would he enter the center of the earth and come out in China on the other side? Faint light seeped round the bend. The black turned to shadowy gray. The steps, Landon noticed, were roughly cut stones like those he'd imagined would lead down into a dungeon. No sooner had he observed this, however, than the stone turned to wood. His footsteps went from taps to soft thumps.

A strange noise came from somewhere. Landon slowed his descent and stopped. He pressed his ear to the rough wood wall. Through the crunching sound of his own blood rushing through his ears, he heard the noise again. *A thousand voices,* he thought, his chest convulsing. The next sound nearly threw him from the wall.

"Heave!"

The shrill voice sounded somewhat near. Landon continued down the steps. He began to wonder. No, it was impossible. Or was it? Could he possibly be inside Ludo's giant tree? If this were true, then right outside would be the Echoing Green.

The passageway became slightly brighter as he reached a landing. Before him ran a short hallway at the end of which appeared an opening to the right and another drop of stairs. To Landon's left was another opening. Landon inched to its edge and peered in. He was looking down a long, roundish passageway with little branches poking into it from the walls and ceiling. Then he realized: It was the inside of a branch. A very large and long branch—extending from Ludo's giant tree.

He heard the strange, distant noise again. "Ohh—whoa!" He knew the voices were really saying, "Ho, Ludo!"

Then from down the branch-corridor, he heard, "Heave!"

"Ho, Ludo," Landon whispered. The words came out reflexively, and Landon could sense the power of the Coin rising and falling outside. He yearned against his better judgment to see it for himself. Suddenly he remembered. *Holly. Oh, no!* He slunk around the corner and began edging his way down the corridor. *If she's watching the Coin, then she may already be under Ludo's spell.* Landon gulped and began to run.

A flash nearly blinded him at the end of the corridor, and Landon scolded himself for glimpsing the Coin. But then he realized it wasn't the Coin at all but the top rim of the sun rising over distant treetops. It was breathtakingly beautiful, and for a moment Landon completely forgot where he was. The sky was turning rosy and bringing out a sparkle from crystalline treetops and the snow-dusted clearing. It was like a magic snow globe waiting to be shaken.

A voice jolted him back to reality.

"I have read the great Coin!"

A gentle murmur resounded far below. Landon couldn't help licking his lips and straining his ears for Ludo's next words.

"And the great Coin says. . .the sun has risen. It's sunup in Wonderwood!"

As the cheering swelled and then quieted, Landon stepped to the opening at the end of the corridor and peered around the edge. His eyes had to adjust to the outside light. Then he looked to his left and bit his tongue to keep from screaming. Wearing a velvety green outfit with what must be a new top hat, Ludo stood with his twiglike arm around the shoulders of a girl with straight blond hair. *Holly! Oh, no.*

Landon pulled back from the doorway and leaned against the wall. He had to think. If Holly was already under Ludo's spell, she wouldn't know she was in danger. She might not want to leave. But Landon had to get her away. The thought of his sister caught in Ludo's clutches would drive him mad.

How could he get her away from him?

Movement caught his eye, and Landon glanced down. At first he thought he was looking at a black slug oozing its way along the floor. Then he noticed that it was flat and had no body. It was a shadow, and it was leaving a trail of shadowy slime that evaporated behind it like the tail of a comet. A very slow and ugly comet.

Landon fought the urge to stomp the thing. Of course, what good would it do to stomp a shadow? It seemed the ugly shape hadn't noticed him, so Landon held himself steady against the wall. The shadow writhed past and then turned. It was heading through the doorway. When Landon could see it no more, he eased himself forward and leaned just enough to peek around the corner. It took a moment, but then he found the shadow squiggling across the deck. It was heading for Ludo and Holly.

"Oh, it was delightful!" Holly squealed. "Such an awesome coin, and heaved so high into the sky. One, two, three times!"

"I am so pleased you take delight in beholding such a sight, me young Hall-lee," Ludo said. "And to know you see all of the numbers—one, two, three! Oh yes, oh yes, that pleases me!" They both clapped. Landon thought he was going to be sick.

Meanwhile, the fat slug had slithered right up to Ludo's coattails, which hung close to the floor. The sun continued to climb. Landon stepped into the doorway. A two-tiered log railing ran across the front of the deck, which ended at either side at a wall of bark. Dangling from a ceiling of bark a ways overhead were circles of glass, each on its own thread.

They were spread at roughly the same height across the deck's length, hanging near eye-level above the railing. As one twinkled and turned, it suddenly struck Landon. They were lenses. He recalled Ludo's voice from the past: *"Up in me tree, me boy, up in me tree. Where I have me lenses, and only I can see, only I can see."*

Attached to the rail near Ludo's right elbow was a crude-looking cone pointing toward the tree and flaring out toward the Echoing Green. It looked precariously uneven, as if the wide end should drop against the rail any moment. But it defied gravity.

Ludo giggled. His bony right hand lifted from the rail, and his fingers spread as if he were about to wave. "And this is the perfect place for you, lassie. For we are the land of Odds! Where numbers are our name and counting is our game!"

If Ludo hadn't tipped back so that his coattails touched the deck, Landon probably would never have noticed. He had nearly forgotten about the slug shadow, but a strange thing happened. Ludo's shadow actually broke away for an instant, merged with Holly's shadow, and then bounded back again. If Landon had blinked, he would have missed it. Even now the shadows behind the two figures seemed somehow denser than they should be. And Landon couldn't be quite sure, but he thought the sluggish shadow was creeping right up Ludo's dark green coat. It was difficult to tell. It seemed to seep into the velvety fabric.

Whatever had happened, Landon had a new image of Ludo as a puppet, and his shadow was the arm of a hand that moved him.

Landon glanced at his own shadow, which stretched back inside the tree. He moved his head slowly. . .and then quickly. His shadow remained perfectly in sync.

Standing in the doorway so close and yet seemingly so far from his sister and her enchanter, Landon almost felt like a shadow himself. Perhaps he was invisible to them. And soundless, too? He was almost ready to test this theory when Ludo's right hand slapped the rail and then clutched it like a claw. His left hand released Holly and clamped onto a dangling lens, bringing it close to his face. His body seemed to stiffen and sag all at once, becoming very taut and tense.

"I cannot believe what mine eyes see. It cannot be. This cannot be!"

"What is it, Ludo?" Holly asked tenderly.

He paid her no attention. Something far below and across the green was bothering him. Landon could almost hear Ludo's nutcracker teeth grinding. "Nutmeg and ratchet," Ludo muttered. "Trumplestump," he said tersely. Pounding the deck with his foot and clapping his hands, he shouted, "Trumplestump! Wagglewhip! Get that animal away from here!"

Animal? Landon's heart leapt. Without thinking, he stepped right out onto the deck. He made it across to the rail and latched a lens to his eye before Ludo took any notice of him. Landon gasped first at the great height he found himself over the perfectly circular Echoing Green spread below. He also noticed sword-length pine needles attached to giant branches above and below and to either side of the deck. At first the lens seemed to distort things, and Landon didn't know what he was looking for. Opening both eyes to scan the far line of trees, he closed his left eye and pressed the lens to his right.

Something was moving very quickly along the rim of the clearing. It was quite dark, and at first its features were indistinguishable. It was racing, almost flying, along the left side of the grass circle. And it was coming their way. Landon had a hard time keeping up, having to continually readjust the lens, which was a tad too small for his eye. He wanted desperately to believe what his heart was telling him, but he needed visual clarification to be sure.

It wasn't only a dark figure. There was something on top of it, riding it. In an instant, the image came into focus, and Landon saw not a shadow but a deep brown horse carrying a goofy-looking passenger. The rider was grinning wildly like a dog with its head out a car window.

Landon gasped and drew his head back from the lens. "Melech," he whispered excitedly.

"And Tardy Hardy, too. How quaint for me and you."

Landon dropped the lens and turned to find Ludo grinning at him. Landon expected an evil or a wicked grin, not a happy-to-see-you grin. But Ludo looked surprisingly happy.

"Well, twirl my goatee and twiddle my thumb! First one guest drops in, and now Second-to-None!"

Ludo extended his hand, and Landon automatically began reaching for it, but then he noticed Ludo's other hand crawling inside his coat and fiddling with something.

"Landon?" Holly peered around Ludo's shoulder. "Landon!"

That moment of distraction was all Ludo needed to whip

out the gold disk on a chain and begin swinging it before Landon's eyes.

"Augh! No!" Landon covered his eyes and looked out at the Echoing Green. Melech and Hardy had cut sharply from the tree line and were racing across the clearing. Confused and worried, Landon grabbed a lens for a closer look. Tiny lines were flying at the horse and rider from the trees to the left, and from the giant tree itself! Landon looked down in horror. Somewhere below, Odds were firing arrows at Melech and Hardy, keeping them from the tree.

"Second-to-None, what is wrong? Look at me and we'll sing a song."

Landon covered his eyes again and flailed wildly with his free hand. "No, Ludo!" he shouted, realizing it sounded very much like the chant, "Ho, Ludo!" He hit a few lenses and felt one strike the back of his head after swinging around. Where had Ludo gone? Landon peeked through his fingers. No one. He lunged for the crude cone and put his mouth to the narrow end. The cone, which was a megaphone, was on a rusty swivel and hinge so he could maneuver it. The metalwork groaned and squeaked. When he had it facing the green, Landon shouted, "Melech! Up here! It's—"

A claw dug into his shoulder and spun him around before he could get his name out.

"Now why did you go and do that? Oh, dear and oh, drat." Ludo wasn't grinning. He shook his head sadly. Holly stood near the doorway, looking rather like a lost kitten.

"She's my sister, and she's with me," said Landon boldly. "Holly, don't listen to him, and don't look—"

"At this?"

The gold fob was up in a glimmer and a flash, and it was all Landon could do to look away and close his eyes.

"Oh, it's too late for her, I'm afraid." Ludo's voice came into Landon's ear hot and heavy. It seemed to be seeping into his brain, almost like the voice was coming from inside Landon's head. This wasn't good. He had to get out of here!

"She's seen my little timepiece, to be sure. But even better, she's seen the rising Coin!"

"Oh, and it's beautiful!" said Holly's voice. "Landon, you were right! It was spectacular! And I got to see it through one of the lenses!"

Great, thought Landon. "I told you it would hypnotize you, Holly! Remember?" Landon cried. And he thought he really was about to cry, he was feeling so hopeless.

"I'm not hypnotized," Holly said with a laugh, but it was a strange and empty sort of laugh that didn't sound like her at all. "But I really cannot wait to see the Coin again. Ludo, when may I? When will it be back?"

Landon's frustration and misery and sadness twirled into a plummeting tailspin. Looking at Ludo's gold fob might provide some relief. The golden shimmer was beautiful, and it was only an appetizer for the great gold Coin. How soon would the Coin be back? Landon wanted to ask, too.

He shook his head madly, trying to fight it off. Ludo's sharp grip loosened on his shoulder and began to gently knead as his voice dripped into Landon's head like syrup.

"That's it, Lan-duhn. Join your sister, and we'll have some fun. We can play all day until the setting sun. Just take a peek at the gold and to my voice listen. . . ."

Landon sighed. He was so tired. His head felt heavy, and

everything was beginning to feel a little dreamy. Why not open his eyes? Why not look at the gold disk? Why not join Holly in the fun? Why not. . .

Just as he began to open his eyes, a sound rose from the green that snapped Landon from his dreamlike state. It was the neighing of a horse. Melech!

Landon fixed his gaze on his feet. "Holly, we've got to get out of here. This is dangerous."

A hand appeared, but it wasn't Holly's. It looked like a claw. With a wavelike motion, the gnarled fingers spread and then flexed. The hand was empty.

"See?" came Ludo's voice. "I put the disk away. There's nothing to fear here, Landon. Why don't you come inside with your sister and me?"

A hint of uneasiness colored Ludo's voice. He sounded a bit anxious.

"I don't want to," said Landon.

"Are you going to just stay out here?" It was Holly's voice. Her feet came into view. Landon glanced up warily at her and then shot a peek at Ludo who, as if caught in some mischievous act, lifted his skinny hands and shrugged his shoulders, smirking.

"See?" said Holly. "He's harmless, Landon. He's fun and smart, actually," she whispered.

Landon glared at her. "Holly! Don't you remember what I told you? He lures you in and then casts a spell with. . .with shimmering gold." Landon scowled at Ludo, whose palms were upraised in a "Who, me?" sort of way.

"Oh, Landon. I don't know what you're talking about. I think the only one under a spell here is you."

Ludo suddenly moved, and Landon flinched, bracing himself. "Come, come, children," Ludo said soothingly. "What is it you want? What is it you seek?" He turned first to Holly and then to Landon, a beseeching look on his face. "Tell your good friend Ludo, and maybe I can help you take a peek."

Holly let out a little giggle. At the sound of it, Landon's heart lifted, but then it quickly sank. "See?" said Holly. "He's cute and funny, Landon. I don't know why you don't care for him."

"Because," Landon said in a voice that almost growled, "he wants to turn your mind to mold and your heart to rust. Or something like that." Landon was remembering the sign he and Melech had seen on the nineteenth Whump Tree before reaching the Echoing Green. Vates had written a message of warning that Hardy had strapped to the tree trunk. The mention of the sign's words affected Ludo, Landon could tell. So he thought he'd try some more.

"Vates posted a warning about him." Landon aimed his thumb in Ludo's direction. "Said he looks neither old nor young and that the Odds are against us. That they may want us dead in here." Landon placed his hand on his heart.

Ludo seemed to be struggling to maintain his friendly veneer. He snickered, but it seemed a nervous snicker to Landon.

"Va–vay–tees." Ludo cringed as he said the name. "Yesss. Putting up those silly signs. He-he! Ha-ha! Come now, children, let me show you some of my toys I have inside." Ludo took hold of Holly's elbow and began leading her toward the doorway.

Holly gave Landon a pleading look. Unfortunately, her expression meant she wanted him to join them. "Toys, Landon. Come on!"

Landon heard Melech neigh somewhere down below. The time to act was now.

"No!" Landon yelled, startling even himself. He lunged for Holly and grabbed her free arm, commencing a tug of war with Ludo on the other side.

"Lan–don!" Holly swayed first one way and then the other way. "Let go of me!"

Instead of letting go, Landon gave an even harder tug. He was holding Holly's jacket sleeve. And as he yanked on it, he realized two things.

First, Holly's jacket was unzipped. Second, as Landon yanked on it, Ludo suddenly let go. This caused Holly to move Landon's way, but only for a moment, because she also twirled and then came right out of her jacket.

Landon found himself stumbling backward with his sister's jacket. He expected to ram against the railing. Instead, he found himself suspended in midair. Landon wanted to shriek, but all he could do was gasp.

He wasn't actually suspended in midair, of course. But in the split second that it took him to tumble backward from the deck and plummet over the side, Landon saw in one horrifying image the reason he had missed the railing. Ludo was standing against the wall with his bony hand on a lever, and the lever was in the down position. As Landon fell, he caught a glimpse of the rail sticking down from the deck. Suddenly the rail was thrust back up with the flip of the lever, and Ludo was giggling like a mean little kid.

His giggles faded quickly as Landon fell.

"Augh!" Landon screamed. Great tree branches flew by in a blur. The pine needles passed just out of reach. Might he somehow use Holly's jacket as a parachute? He was just getting it untangled when the ground came too quickly into view.

Chapter Six

Before Landon hit the ground, he thought he caught a glimpse of Holly leaning out over the rail high in the tree. Or else he imagined it. For when he looked up a moment later, she was nowhere to be seen.

But Landon never did hit the ground. Instead, he landed in two strong arms that, after catching him, gave him a gentle squeeze and then deposited him on a thick, cloth saddle.

"Gotcha!" said a voice behind him.

"Oof!" said Landon. He was thinking "Thank you" and "I can't believe I just did that," but "Oof!" was the best he could manage at the moment.

Swish! Swish-swish! Three arrows zipped past.

Landon ducked and grabbed hold of the rein lying across the horse's back. "Just like old times, eh, Melech? Hyah!"

Melech reared up, neighing and cycling his hoofs through the air. He came down with a thud and shot off at a gallop beneath the high limbs of the great pine tree and into the forest. Landon noticed twinkling lights among the boughs and needles. "Fireflies," he said, remembering the slumbering insects inside their hard, clear bubbles. Strangely, they had glowed during the day but faded with the night. Landon craned his neck to look back, but the observation deck with Holly and Ludo was long gone from sight.

"We can't leave her there with him!" Landon had to shout over rushing wind and galloping hoofs.

"It's good to see you, too, young Landon." Melech cut sharply at a tree trunk before hurdling a fallen log.

"I know," said Landon, who was feeling an odd mix of emotion and exhilaration. He patted Melech's neck and almost wanted to cry for joy at being reunited with his old friend. "I'm glad to see you, Melech. Really glad. And thanks, Hardy," he added over his shoulder. "I just—how did you know I was here?"

Thwack!

Landon flinched as an arrow split a branch overhead. *That was close!*

"D—didn't kno—ow," Hardy said, his voice bouncing as Melech stutter-stepped and turned. "Just posting a sign."

"From Vates?" Landon's heart gave a leap.

"Who else?" Hardy grinned, his teeth poking the air in several directions.

Landon's joy was fleeting. "We can't leave her behind—my sister."

Melech strained against the reins, forging ahead as Landon began jerking back to wheel around. Finally, Melech relented and slowed, though he didn't turn back. He paused, panting, behind a thick tree. Arrows could be heard splintering wood from the other side.

"The wisest course may be to return undercover," said Melech. "The Odds are against us, and their supply of stick weapons seems endless."

"But they never actually hit us," Landon explained. "Remember our escape last time? From Maple Tree Max and then from here?" He was thinking of his and Melech's journey through Wonderwood on his last visit.

Melech craned his neck, studying Landon and exchanging looks with Hardy. Landon found his gaze bouncing between them. After much silence (save the piercing of wood and the splashing of dirt from so many arrows), Landon said slowly, "What?"

Melech sighed and stared at the forest. "Some have found their mark, young Landon. Show him, Hardy."

Landon could sense the gravity in Melech's voice. Hardy leaned forward and stretched out his arm.

"Skin scrape, skin scrape, nudding but skin scrapes." He had pulled up his sleeve, which itself had been ripped and torn in various places, and was turning his arm this way and that, pointing out scars and scratches and a couple half-healed wounds. Landon could hardly believe it.

"Those are from arrows? Not from branches or bushes?"

Melech softly neighed and bowed his head. Two welts stretched along his right shoulder. Landon winced but then reached out to gently stroke Melech's coat alongside the nasty scars. Melech's skin fluttered at his touch, but he made no complaint.

Hardy worked his fingers through two holes and wriggled them like little legs. "Dey always did hate dis shirt," he said.

"The Odds have gotten worse since you left, Landon. Or

their aim has gotten better. Things have gotten darker. Things only Vates could explain."

"If things are worse," said Landon, "I really don't want to leave Holly here." He hugged her jacket and hoped she wasn't too cold without it. "What will happen to her?"

Something rustled overhead, and a leaf came fluttering down. Landon started, fearing an Odd might be above them preparing to shoot or to send down a flurry of helicopter seeds. Instead Landon heard the sweetest sound in the world. A bird sang two notes. "Twee-too. Twee-too."

Landon looked up but saw nothing but tree.

"Epops will keep an eye on her as much as is possible," said Melech.

"Epops?"

"Vay-dees's birdie," said Hardy. "Here, liddle birdie! Dwee-dwee!" He held out his arm like a branch, and the most beautiful little bird alighted, twisting its emerald head.

"Epops," said Landon.

The bird glanced sideways at him and blinked as if it understood. Landon suddenly realized that this was the bird he had heard singing in the early morning when he, Melech, Hardy, and Ditty were heading toward Vates's place in the foothills. It was the only animal other than Melech and the thousands of sleeping fireflies present in all of Wonderwood. Its simple song brightened the entire forest. With this bird around, it seemed everything would be okay.

Landon held out his arm. Epops hopped to it and clutched the sleeve of his jacket. The bird was so light, Landon could hardly tell it was there. As Epops skittered up to his shoulder and then burst into the air with a flash of green and white feathers, it was as if it had whispered into Landon's ear, *She'll be okay. I'll let you know when the time is right. Good-bye!*

Then the bird was gone.

C h a p t e r   S e v e n

omething was peculiar about the forest. Landon liked to figure things out, so he put his mind to work on it. He studied their surroundings, and it finally came to him. He was so excited he nearly elbowed Hardy in the ribs.

"The leaves," said Landon. "They're still in the trees, but it's like they're frozen or something."

When a breeze whistled through the branches, the leaves did not whisper or make their usual, wonderful whooshing sound. They rattled. And sometimes a light cool powder of snow sprinkled down.

"A dark, cold season is coming," said Melech. "Indeed, it has already begun."

A crunching, slobbering noise came from behind, and Landon turned to spy Hardy chomping an apple. Hardy paused, grinned, and offered Landon a bite. Landon shook his head.

"Some hot cider would be good about now," he said. "But

a hard, cold apple? No thanks."

Hardy shrugged and gnawed another piece.

They had escaped the flying arrows, and Melech seemed more relaxed as he galloped through the woods. They reached the river in no time, and it dawned on Landon that they had been following a sort of trail.

"You've traveled this way a lot," he said.

Melech drew up at the top of the bank overlooking the expanse of flowing water. A cloud of mist hung over the river. Melech snorted, adding his own puffs of mist to the chill air. Landon touched his own ears and realized they'd gone nearly numb. His cheeks felt tingly, while his hair was actually damp with sweat. He felt both warm and cold at the same time.

"Around Echoing Green, we never follow the same path twice—to better dodge the arrows. Once we're a safe distance away, I know the route I like to take."

"Can do it wid blinders on," said Hardy tapping Landon's shoulder. "Dis horsy got good sense."

Hardy suddenly dismounted and stepped into the high grass. Landon remembered Lily Pad Crossing, although the sign was no longer jutting up from the bank. "Stones?" he called after Hardy.

"Drow away!" Hardy shouted back, lifting his hands. Hardy then lifted the bottom hem of his shirt (he had no coat on despite the cool weather) and bent down to forage for rocks.

Landon jumped down and joined him. First he filled his jacket pockets. Then he began filling one of Holly's jacket pockets, but he felt something inside. Jamming the stone he was holding (it was a nice hard gray one he couldn't wait to throw into the water) into one of his own pockets, he reached back into Holly's pockets. He found four objects: two in each of her pockets.

One pocket held a pen and tiny notebook, and in the other he found a calculator and a tape measure. Landon grinned. She didn't like to just count things; she was now getting into measuring things and making calculations. A page in her notebook revealed a rough sketch or diagram of a pillar or perhaps a building. He also saw a circle with a line running from its center to the edge like one spoke of a wheel. Outside the circle, a calculation had been scribbled involving numbers and that funny shape with two legs and a flat hat that Landon recognized as the Greek letter *pi*. He had no idea what it was doing amid a bunch of numbers, however.

"She wants to be an architect," he said to himself. "Or an engineer."

Already, she was a better drawer than he was; he could tell just by looking at the simple design she'd put down. It appeared almost three-dimensional.

"You coming? Or want to wait here?"

Hardy sat astride Melech with a load of rocks bulging out of his shirt. Part of Hardy's own slightly bulging belly hung out from beneath the makeshift rock-pouch he had clamped to his chest with one fist. Landon shuddered not at Hardy's belly bulge but because the bare skin reminded him of how chilly it was.

"Hang on," said Landon. He replaced Holly's items in her pockets, rolled up her jacket, and tucked it under his arm, doing his best to make a pouch of his own jacket. He filled it till its weight nearly pulled it from his fingers. As he waddled over to Melech, the horse bent its front knees so Landon could more easily climb aboard. "Thanks," said Landon panting.

"Not a problem," said Melech curving his neck to gaze at Landon. "It is good to see you, young Landon. I feared—well, I wondered if you had been banished from this game."

"Oh, no," said Landon. "I just, well, I can only come here on special occasions, I think."

"And this is a special occasion," said Melech, "having you back again."

Landon wanted to hug Melech's neck and stroke his thick black mane, but then he would have spilled his cargo. So he merely sighed and nodded, clambering to get his leg over and his body sitting up. He'd spied Hardy's jack-o'-lantern grin from the corner of his eye and turned to grin back. Hardy's smile broadened even more, and he punctuated it with a wink.

That's when Landon remembered his flashlight. He felt his smile fade as he faced forward, drooping his head. The strap must have slipped from his wrist when he'd lunged and grabbed for Holly's jacket.

"I miss her," said Landon. "It feels bad leaving her back there. Are you sure she'll be all right?" He didn't know if he was asking Melech or Hardy or asking the question rhetorically, which he knew meant there was no answer expected from anyone. Sort of like when his mom asked him, "Oh, what on earth will I do with you?"

Hardy answered anyway. And despite him sounding like he was smiling and possibly drooling (he made a lot of sniffling and slurping noises between words), his answer comforted Landon.

"Epops," he said slurpingly. "Dat bird keep good eye on her. It knows. And if she get into trouble? *(Sniff!)* Den Epops fly straight to us. But I don't dink Ludo want to hurt her. Not yet." He belched so powerfully Landon felt a little relieved himself.

"Not yet?" Landon glanced across his shoulder.

Hardy shook his head. "She filling in now. . .for Ditty."

"Oh," said Landon slowly, "great." But it didn't feel great at all. He wanted to ask about the shadows he'd seen and the cold darkness coming that Melech had spoken of, but Melech was beginning to shift his weight restlessly. He pawed the ground and snorted. "Ready, you two?"

"On the count of three," said Landon, eyeing the misty water ahead.

"On the count of which number?" said Melech, lifting his head.

"Three," Landon said tensely. "Three!"

Melech reared up and then thundered down the slope. "Three—hee—hee—hee!" hollered Landon, and Melech whinnied in response.

Landon threw out a stone. A gray circle appeared flush on the water's surface, growing until it was a ten-foot-wide pad of stone. Melech leaped from the shore, and Landon hurled another stone, and another, and another. It was exhilarating crossing the river this way, and as cold as Landon's ears and nose and cheeks were, he wouldn't have traded the ride for anything. Even a warm hat and scarf.

Hardy took over halfway across, and Landon could immediately tell that the Odd was well practiced at this. The first time they'd gone over with Melech on stone pads (Hardy,

Landon, and Ditty had been riding Melech, and that story is recorded in *Landon Snow and the Auctor's Riddle*), Hardy had thrown away all his stones too early so that they barely made it across without plunging into the river. Now, Hardy seemed completely at ease, giggling (and drooling) as he leisurely lobbed one stone and then another, switching between his right arm and his left, tossing sideways or high overhead. Each stone was perfectly placed so Melech hardly had to break his stride. All in all, it was one beautifully orchestrated ride. When they reached the opposite bank, Melech galloped to the top.

Feeling much lighter and damper and colder than ever, they headed into the woods. Tiny bits of water dripped from Landon's face. They were traveling an even better-worn path on this side of the river. Though Melech kept to an easy trot, Landon knew they were making good time. He thought of the door in the hill bordered by windows and all the books inside. Would Vates be working on another poem or riddle or strange message? Then Landon thought about someone else.

His teeth began to chatter, so he clenched them. Trying to sound nonchalant, he asked, "So, uh, how is she doing, anyway?" Despite the outside temperature, Landon suddenly felt very warm inside.

Melech's head bobbed, and he snorted, but Hardy did the talking.

"No news from Epops is good news, in dis case," he said.

"Oh, right," said Landon. "But, I mean, well, how is she doing? You know." He awkwardly cleared his throat. "I mean Ditty."

"Ha!" Hardy clapped, and Landon jumped. "Dat Ditty

girl ask about dis boy every da–day." Landon felt a sharp slap
on his back when Hardy said "boy." And Landon's face blazed
with fire. It felt like someone was clamping his throat and
pressing on his heart—but in a good way.

Landon had to work up the courage to say it. "She asks
about me?"

"Well, she does when she's not nosing de books. Looking
at all de marks and dings."

Another sort of wonder tickled Landon's heart. "She's
learning to read?"

"Vates teach her every da–day. What a spoil of time."
Hardy whistled and then said, "Shash now. Dere it comes."

Melech had eased to an easy walk as the forest dribbled
away around them. They reached the end of the wood, and
before them swelled the foothills. The sky had thickened and
grayed to almost ash. But it hadn't quite hidden the grand
mountain looming behind the hills. It was the first time
Landon had seen the peak this trip, and he was amazed that
he'd forgotten about it until now. For some reason, this thought
made him feel a little guilty, as if he should apologize to the
craggy climb of rock and tree.

But then he forgot about it again. For there was Vates's
door at the base of a nicely rounded hill, and on either side
of the door shone a window marked with crisscrossed lines. It
was like seeing something out of a dream from long ago. It all
looked so much the same, except the sky hung much heavier
and everything was lightly dusted with snow.

The world seemed to grow stiller and more silent with
each step. The snow cover was too thin to crunch, yet it
softened Melech's hoofs like fine powder. Landon found

himself holding his breath. Did they need to advance on the hill with such stealth? What were they trying to do? Sneak up on the old man and startle him with a—

"Surprise, surprise! Uncork the ginger ale and break out the pumpkin pies!"

Melech had gone rigid, Hardy had yelped, and Landon was still holding his breath before they all melted in laughter.

"Come on and come in! And, oh, my sweet mountain air—but it's good to see you here finally, young man. Yes, of course we've been expecting you. Well, I have anyway. Come on and get some warmth."

It was Vates, of course. He'd burst out from behind the rough wooden hatch like a mad jack-in-the-box. Actually, a happy jack-in-the-box. All white hair and long beard and twinkling eyes and gesturing hands, which were now all they could see of him waving them in.

"I hate it when he does that," said Melech dryly, though Landon thought he detected a trace of humor in the horse's usually staid voice.

"How does dat man know?" said Hardy in exasperation. "Does he sit all day at de window?"

Landon was still catching his breath and fighting a giggle, even as his heart continued to race from the sudden thrill. "Boy, he got us. He got us good." He laughed and shook his head. "My dad would say that just took a minute off my life. And I think it might have."

"Next time," said Hardy as he and Landon dismounted, "we go de back of de hill and den—pop!—right by de window. Bounce de old man straight to de galley."

Landon laughed heartily. Even before stepping inside, he

was feeling warm and tingly all over. Deep down, he couldn't shake the mysterious yet wonderful feeling that somehow he was coming home—to a second sort of home.

"Wait there," Vates commanded, holding up his palm.

Landon paused on the threshold as Hardy and Melech traipsed inside. He wanted so much to follow and see all the books and catch sight of. . .her. But he waited.

Vates reappeared carrying a lantern. Landon was disappointed to discover it had a real flame. He had hoped to see a glowing firefly floating in a bubble. Vates's lantern did have something strange about it, however. The back of the inside was curved and shiny like a mirror. And atop the lantern was a concave gold disk, also very shiny. Light from the flame must have been shooting up and into the top disk somehow, where it was projected out in a beam more intense than Landon's flashlight produced.

"Hold still," said Vates. "Goodness and graciousness but they're all over you."

"What are you—augh! Get 'em off me! Get 'em off!"

At first Landon thought they were giant black leeches from the river. Then he realized how flat they were and that they had no substance. They had no bodies, only shadows.

Vates sighed as he directed the lantern's beam across Landon's back from his shoulders down, and then down the back of each leg. It was all Landon could manage not to jump or bolt or flail like an electrified wire. Panting, he merely watched as the shadows silently crept back toward the woods. Every now and then, one would vanish in a dip or behind a bush or as it momentarily blended with a real shadow. Then it would appear again, slinking toward the wood.

"Graciousness and goodness." Vates held up the lantern, shining it back and forth across the lawn as if he were washing the slithery things away. "You had a good dozen of them on you, son. What were you doing? Climbing Ludo's tree?"

"Actually, I was inside the tree," said Landon.

Vates stopped in midpivot with the lantern like an old lighthouse that had run out of fuel. He slowly cast his gaze upon Landon. "You were inside, eh?" From the twinkle in his eye and the twitch at the corner of his lip, the old man almost seemed impressed.

Landon nodded, wondering if it was yet safe for him to move.

"Then that's where they found you all right. Those snakes don't get out so much in the daylight." He made one more sweep with the lantern and, seeming satisfied, turned to the doorway.

Landon still didn't move. "Vates," he whispered. It felt like he had a guilty secret to share, though he didn't know why it should feel guilty.

"Yes?" Vates held the lantern by a chain so that it swung below his fist like a hanging lamp at sea. "What is it?" Vates tilted his head and arched a white eyebrow.

"Well," said Landon, "they—I mean those shadow things—might have come from somewhere else."

"Oh?" The lantern slowed its swing and gently twirled until it came to rest on Landon like a searchlight.

Landon squinted and blinked. "I mean I saw them first, well, up in my world."

Vates sighed, and the slight movement caused the beam to glide away from Landon's face. "That's not unexpected, of course. Malus Quidam has infected all of the Auctor's creation." He seemed to be speaking to himself. "What is surprising is that you saw him. Yes, that is most puzzling and most interesting. . . .

"Landon." Vates glanced sharply as if just remembering Landon was there. "There is much to discuss, and it seems there may be less time than I thought. There's always time for refreshments, though. Do come in! And welcome—again—to my humble dwelling." Vates prodded Landon in the back as if knowing he needed a nudge.

Landon still felt quite jittery about having all those shadows latched to his jacket. How long had they been there? And what exactly did they—or could they—do to him? Giving one last shudder from his head to his knees, Landon stepped into the side of the hill where Vates's home was built. It took Landon only a second to spot Ditty. She was sitting at the rough wooden table with her arms crossed upon it. A large book lay open before her. She lifted her nose from the pages and set her two big eyes upon Landon.

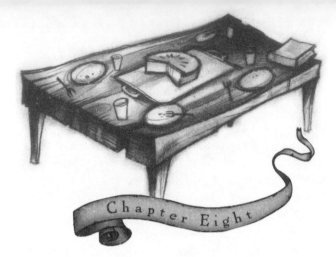

Landon wondered if he was floating in a dream.

Ditty had smiled at him, but his initial happiness fell as a look of concern drew down her face. Did she see something hideous behind him? Another shadow leech or something?

"Don't you remember?" she asked. Her voice slightly trembled.

Landon had taken a hopeful step toward the table. Now he lurched to a stop. "Remember what?"

Her eyes glistened and softened. Landon thought he might faint. "Me," she whispered. "You remember, don't you?"

Landon couldn't believe his ears. His mouth went dry, and his face radiated heat. "Of course I do," he said finally, blinking. "Yes, I remember."

The most wonderful smile lit her face. Then she suddenly frowned and looked hard at her book, tracing with her finger. Her hand stopped. She nodded. Then she glanced up, smiling as if nothing had happened. "Didn't want to lose my place," she said. "This is a good book."

Vates strolled out from the kitchen—or galley, as Hardy called it—bearing a tray laden with food and drink. "Ales and pie, pie and ales. Makes a man spry, it never fails."

As Vates set down the tray, Ditty scooped up her book, keeping her finger pressed between the pages. Hardy scraped a chair back and sat down with a thud, and Vates wagged a finger at him. "Our guest first, Hardy. There's plenty for all."

Hardy sagged his shoulders and sighed, licking his lips as he glared at Landon. Melech stood to the right of the galley's entryway in a nook Landon didn't remember from before. "Is that new?" he asked indicating the hollowed-out space.

Melech snorted and nodded as Vates set a bucket of water before him along with another pail full of what appeared to be oats.

Vates brushed off his hands. "It's nice, eh? A little add-on for Melech here." He patted Melech's neck. "A good horse needs a spot of his own. And the bump outside the hill is hardly noticeable. We did have to push it out and lay some new sod. Now, Landon, if you please, help yourself. Or poor Hardy will be slobbering over everything."

The table had been shoved farther out from the back wall, and another chair had been added, as if they had been expecting him. Landon sat to Ditty's right, facing the wall, with Hardy opposite her. As soon as Landon had a triangle of pie on his platter and a mug of ginger ale in his hand (the drink was room temperature, but it went down deliciously), Vates took the chair nearest the wall and sat down.

"So tell me, Landon, after you swallow, of course. Do tell

me all about your adventure so far." Vates leaned on the table, pressing his palms together as if he were praying. He gazed intently at Landon, and though Landon really didn't think there was too much to tell, the way Vates listened to him, he might have been relating the most fantastic story ever told.

Landon started with the moving bookcase in Grandpa Karl's study and then mentioned seeing the first strange shadow. Vates's eyes widened, and he interlaced his fingers and rested his chin on them. "Before the shadow and before the bookcase opened, what exactly were you doing?"

Landon thought for a moment. "Reading the Bible—well, it was moving on its own, turning to different pages. I read the underlined words."

Vates was nodding and making *mm* and *mm-hmm* sounds. "And what did those words say?"

"I don't remember exactly. But they were about darkness and light. And good and evil. Oh! And the first one was Adam and Eve and the serpent and the tree and all that."

"This is found in the Auctor's Book."

Landon waited, wondering if it was a question or a statement. Finally, he said, "Yes. The Bible."

"And then you saw the shadow slipping back into the tunnel?"

"Well, it went behind the bookcase, so—"

"Mm," said Vates closing his eyes. "Mm-hmm. Indeed."

Hardy prodded Landon with a gentle elbow and gestured toward the remaining two pieces of pie. Landon shrugged and said, "Go ahead. I'm full." With his mouth hanging open, Hardy then gazed at Vates, who appeared to be meditating or praying. His eyes were still closed, and his mouth was hidden behind his folded hands. Hardy began to pant and smack his lips. Finally, Ditty said, "Just eat, Hardy. You know he doesn't mind."

Hardy fixed her with a glare but then seemed to forget all about her as he shoveled a piece into his mouth and began to chew.

Vates asked Landon to continue. He didn't interrupt him again until Landon got to the part where he had leaped from the balcony in Ludo's tree.

"You grabbed your sister's jacket and jumped with it."

"Yes," said Landon.

"And if Holly had come down with you—who would have caught her?"

Landon opened his mouth to answer, but all that came out was a tiny *uh* sound. And then another one. His forehead suddenly felt heavy, pushing down his eyebrows. He glanced at the table, ashamed and embarrassed. "I guess I thought I would land on Melech and Hardy would catch her." Was he making this up? It had happened so suddenly.

Vates sat back and sighed. "You would've landed on Melech. From that great height. No, Landon. It was meant to be this way. You were spurred by a feeling—a gut reaction— and an unconscious thought." He was nodding. "Yes, this was meant to be."

"Do you really think Holly's all right. . .with him?" Landon earnestly searched Vates's face.

The old man smiled. "At this point, it's better that she's there than here."

"What do you mean?"

"She's a distraction; she'll be safe. At least for another day."

"A distraction?" repeated Landon. "Another day? I don't understand."

Vates looked at Ditty, then Hardy, then over at Melech, and finally back at Landon. It struck Landon that these four had spent some time together in his absence. They were like a family of sorts. Vates the grandfather, Hardy the goofy uncle, Ditty the granddaughter, and Melech, well, the horse.

"For some time, Ludo's powers have been weakening. And the reason is, they're not his powers—they're Malus Quidam's."

Landon felt an eerie chill at the mention of that name, though he didn't feel afraid. At least not in Vates's house.

"Malus Quidam," Landon said, testing the sound of these foreign words on his tongue. "Who is that?"

Everyone shifted uncomfortably and turned to Vates. Hardy coughed and spit a small piece of pie onto his plate, which he immediately slurped back up and swallowed. Even Melech had raised his nose from a bucket and swung his head Vates's way. Landon began to feel a little nervous.

"Malus Quidam is the prince of darkness. The evil one. He is rarely, if ever, seen—if he even deserves to be called a 'he.' 'It' would be more fitting. But his imprints are everywhere. Sadly, his influence is quite pervasive in both our worlds."

"Imprint," said Landon. "Like a stamp?"

Vates nodded. "Movable stamps. Or shadows."

Landon gasped and felt a chill climb his spine. He straightened his back. It took him a moment to breathe. "Those are all from. . .*it*?" He suddenly didn't want to say or hear that name again.

"His shadows are part of him. But they're not all of him."

Landon swallowed. He couldn't resist searching the corners of the room and the dark space behind the bookshelf opposite the window. "Where is. . .*all* of him?" He tried to sound calm despite the clenched feeling in his stomach.

Vates leaned over the table. His eyes studied Landon's face but then drifted down, softening with tiredness and something else. Sadness perhaps. "The prince of darkness dwells in the blackest place of all. Where there is no light, ever. Not even a glimmer. It's a place of madness and loneliness and pain."

"Why would he want to live there?"

Vates's gaze lifted gently. "Nothing lives there, for it is death. It's the place of death. The Auctor creates life and gives light to live by. Malus Quidam seeks to destroy life and cover everything with the darkness of death. Even our thoughts get twisted by his lies."

Landon thought of the bookwyrmen in the library and the lying book that had deceived Holly. Then there was that creepy whisper Landon had heard when the steel grate had momentarily turned to smoke. "Come in. . .come in!" The memory made his stomach turn.

A finger tapped him twice on the nose. Landon blinked and turned his head. Ditty was smiling at him. Being here with his friends, in this place, made Landon suddenly smile despite himself. "It's good to see you. . .all. . .again," he said, looking at each of them. "I only wish Holly were here, too."

"Epops will keep an eye on her."

Landon looked at Vates and found himself nodding. "So

she'll be all right." And in his heart, Landon somehow knew that she would be.

Vates sighed. "We have much to plan and prepare."

"To plan and prepare?" Landon asked blankly.

Vates smiled. "To attack the shadows of Malus Quidam."

Landon swallowed. It felt like two large hands were compressing his chest. It was difficult to breathe. Hardy, too, was apparently startled. He bumped a mug and spilled ginger ale, which fizzed on the floor before soaking into the wood. Hardy looked down at it. "Drats and fiddlesticks. What a waste."

"Attack?" said Landon in a small voice. "How. . .what. . .I mean, they're shadows." He felt his eyebrows pinching together.

Vates's expression hardly changed, but his eyes drew Landon in and then directed him to follow their gaze to the book lying before Ditty's crossed arms on the table. Ditty closed the book, and Landon saw the lettering flash as the light passed over it. *The Book of*"—Landon tilted his head—"*Illumi. . .nation. The Book of Illumination.*"

Vates drew in a long, deep breath. "That is our means of attack."

Landon thought about it. Did he mean the book or. . .what? "Illumination," said Landon. He looked up and met Vates's gaze over the table. "Light," said Landon. "We attack shadows with light."

The old man's eyes took on an extra glimmer. "It's the only way. The trick is we must not only attack. We must surround and ensnare the shadows so that they cannot escape. We must capture Malus Quidam with light. And that, Landon Snow, is why I believe you are here."

Chapter Nine

*S*ure, Landon thought. *I'm here to capture the evil one of darkness with light. Right.* He grinned at Ditty, but she had opened the book and was reading, mouthing words silently to herself. Apparently the preparation had begun.

"It may sound impossible," said Vates, "but it's not. For we are not alone. You were called to see visions, and I was called to dream dreams. Remember?"

Landon felt foolish for grinning. He tried to look serious. "Visions and dreams," he said quietly.

"Yes," Vates said. "And not only old men like me and young men like you, but daughters, too."

Landon had read the verses in Bartholomew G. Benneford's ancient Bible many times. He closed his eyes to picture the passages in his mind. " 'And your sons and daughters shall prophesy.' " He opened his eyes and stared at Vates in astonishment. "Holly? Will she prophesy something?"

"Well!" Vates was laughing. "It will be exciting to see, won't it? Perhaps she'll play a part in your vision or my dream. We'll find out as we plan and prepare for battle."

"You know," Ditty said, lifting her eyes from the book, "it was the very first thing the Auctor spoke into existence."

Landon looked at her and waited. Finally, he asked, "What was?"

She peered at him, wrinkling her nose. "You know."

Landon blinked. Looking at Ditty's face only helped him draw a blank.

Ditty made a slight snorting noise in mock exasperation. "This," she said, and she flipped the cover of the book over and pointed to the final word in the title.

Landon looked. "Illumination?"

Ditty giggled and shook her hair back and forth. Then she looked at him, her big eyes crinkling at the corners. "Yeah, same thing." Landon didn't understand until she said, " 'Light.' "

"Right, right," he said in rhyming echo. His face felt warm at his slowness. Why did Ditty have this effect on him? It felt like bright light—illumination—heating his skin.

"So." Landon turned his attention to Vates. The old man's visage helped Landon think clearly, unlike Ditty's. "We need to plan and prepare, huh?"

Vates's eyes were twinkling at him. "First we will eat lunch. It's not good to plan or prepare anything on an empty stomach."

"Hear, hear!" Hardy stood and clapped, bumping the table and causing ale to slosh in the mugs. He sat back down. "Eat to plan. Plan to eat. Hear, hear, hear!"

It seemed as though they had just eaten pie. Yet more

time had slipped by than Landon was aware. After eating vegetable stew—and drinking more ginger ale, which was followed by a rousing round of burps, Melech's being the most boisterous—everyone went outside for fresh air. The sky had grown overcast and seemed to hang with a flat gray sheen. Snowflakes were falling. A noticeable chill penetrated the air, but it was something else that caused Landon to shiver.

His breath came out in a small cloud. "What are those?"

Beneath the low gray clouds, darker shapes were moving. At first it looked like a huge flock of crows, their bodies and wings overlapping to create an almost seamless black carpet. Somehow, Landon could tell they were not crows. For one thing, there was no cawing. In fact, no sound came from the mysterious, dark shifting mass. With no other words to describe the sight, Landon offered, "Are they bats?" He thought bats flew rather soundlessly, at least to human ears.

"Oh no," Ditty said, a worried look on her face. "I remember this happening before. This is just like—Oh! I don't want to see this!" She stopped abruptly and turned and ran inside.

Landon swung his head around to watch her go. Then he turned from the closing door back to the forest and the dreadfully darkening sky.

"Night is descending early this bleak day," said Vates thoughtfully. He was clutching the head of his walking stick with both hands, leaning on it, appearing to brace himself against something. "More and more shadows. He's moving faster than I had anticipated."

Vates turned and gazed at Landon a long time, an unreadable expression on his face. Landon thought he heard something. A whispery voice sounded inside his head, yet he felt certain it was coming from outside. From up above.

As more black shapes fluttered silently overhead, Landon heard the strange voice again. His skin tingled as if pulled by a thousand tiny tweezers. The sky had become a thick blanket of shifting dusk. And in the dimness, Vates suddenly seemed farther away. Was he walking backward? Drifting somehow toward the fading hill? Or was Landon moving into the darkness of the woods?

"Remember, Landon." Vates's voice seemed so far away. Landon wanted to cry out to him, when he heard him again in the faintest of whispers. "Though you walk through the valley of shadows, you need not fear. Remember, you are not alone. Prepare yourself!"

Landon's heart pounded. *Vates!* He wanted to cry out. *Come back! Don't leave me out here!* The old man was nowhere to be seen.

Landon shivered more from fear than from cold. He hugged his arms to his chest. Hadn't Hardy and Melech come out as well? Where were they? What had Ditty remembered that had scared her off? *She knows something,* Landon thought. *Why didn't she warn me? Or is this a test that she has already passed?* He was wishing he had run back to the hill with her.

Something moved. Landon gasped, straining his eyes. Something slithered along the ground. Landon jumped, afraid to touch the thing. As it passed, he noticed nothing but a sliding patch of darkness. Then others appeared, many stretched out like snakes. But they were only shadows. Landon held his breath and tried to remain calm. *If I stay still,*

maybe they'll all pass me by and leave me alone. Except that
they just kept coming. Soon it seemed the earth itself was a
wriggling mass of shadows. Landon wanted desperately to
run, but as he looked about, there was nowhere to go. The
black moving shadows were everywhere.

Something else moved. It was a quicker action, almost
as if a large dog had leaped from behind a tree. "Melech?"
Landon tried hopefully. "Is that you?" His voice was absorbed
by the enveloping darkness, swallowed by silence.

"Watch you!"

"What?" Landon whirled about. Who said that? The voice
had come from two places at once as if spoken from two or
more mouths.

Woof! Hiss!

Landon spun around again. Another figure leapt from
behind a tree, and then another and another. There was a
pack of them. They looked like black wolves except they had
no bodies. They were merely shapes that seemed to suck away
the light from anything they passed over. They were wolf-
shaped black holes. One of them approached as the others
circled. Landon could only stare.

"A boy with a vision, are you?" The voice came from the
approaching wolf and then echoed from surrounding wolves.
"Well, I would like to offer you a grander vision, Landon
Snow. A much grander vision indeed."

The black wolf was rubbing Landon's legs like a cat.
Landon felt no fur nor warmth nor muscle nor bones.
Wherever the wolf stood or rubbed against him, Landon felt
absolutely nothing at all. Neither could he see his legs behind
or through the creature-shadow. It was as if he had no legs at

all. The sensation made him feel as if he might drop to the ground at any moment.

"A grander vision, do you understand?" The wolf looked up at him, but it was only a blank black shape.

"No," Landon said weakly, surprised to hear his own voice. "What are you talking about?"

Something inside Landon told him not to listen to this creature or the voice or whatever this was. But the more the wolf rubbed him, the more curious he became. Landon was beginning to feel quite proud of himself for not running like a scaredy-cat as Ditty had.

The black wolf rubbed. "Another prophecy was told of you. Do you remember?"

Landon thought hard. A prophecy had been told about him? Now he really wanted to know more. "I. . .don't remember. What prophecy?"

The wolf growled and purred, though Landon felt nothing against his legs.

"Oh, I'm sure that you do. But let me remind you. Last time you were here, the words were spoken. You were hailed as Second-to-None. Did you not think about that? And if you're Second-to-None, then you are really Number One."

Landon laughed. He was not feeling himself at all. He wasn't sure if he had actually laughed or if the creature had laughed and somehow caused a tickling feeling inside Landon's ribs.

"Yes," Landon heard himself saying. "They called me Second-to-None."

"And how did that make you feel?"

Landon smiled. He was feeling quite weird at the

moment; that's for sure. "Good," he said. "I liked it."

"Yes. It was good. It is good. And now for the grander vision. Are you ready?"

Something inside pulled at Landon, telling him to say no. But some other part of him opened his mouth and said, "Yes."

"You could be the Reader of the Coin and the Leader of the Odds. You can be, Landon Snow. If you only do one thing. Do you agree?"

The other wolves closed in. The snake shadows on the ground paused, and the bat shadows in the air hovered. Landon imagined the Coin rising into a twilit sky, high over the Echoing Green, while he followed it through the lenses from Ludo's tree. But wait. That could be *his* tree! And those would be *his* lenses!

"Only I can see," said Landon quietly. He thought of gazing down upon the giant catapult spoon with the rope-pullers standing at the ready. Excitement growing in his heart, Landon heard himself shout, "Heave!" He let the word hang in the air, savoring the feel and the sound and the power of giving a command.

"Ho, Landon Snow!"

"Heave!"

"Ho, Landon Snow!"

"Heave!"

"Ho, Landon Snow!"

A thousand voices had shouted all around him. "They listen to me," Landon said, feeling his heart pounding like a hammer. "They all listen to me!"

"So then," said the voice, now spiraling around his head and twisting lightly about his neck, "do you agree?"

Landon wanted to say yes. He was ready to say it. Why wasn't he saying it? Something no stronger than a twitch was holding him back. "Do I agree—to what exactly?"

A hissing sound bounced from ear to ear. The voice faintly murmured, "Follow me."

"I don't know," Landon said weakly. Why didn't he just give in? What would be wrong about following a voice?

"Follow me, and I will grant your vision and fulfill your dream. You will rule and command the Odds. Think of it!"

Something hard was in Landon's hand. It felt like the knobby end of a thick branch. Vates's walking stick! How had it gotten here? Landon glanced around. He could see only the shadows, an army of eerie dark shapes. Landon clutched the staff. *I'm not alone,* he thought, and he wasn't thinking of Vates. *The Auctor is with me.*

"No," said Landon, squeezing the ball of wood.

The shadows seemed to silently gasp and draw back. A moment later, they closed in again. The darkness grew thicker.

"Though I walk through the valley," Landon said. His mouth was going dry. "The valley—of shadows, I am not afraid." Moisture dampened his armpits and the palms of his hands. Landon licked his lips. "His staff is with me, and he comforts me, and he is with me!"

Landon closed his eyes as the wolves leaped at him and the bats swooped and the snakes zipped like arrows. But when he opened his eyes again, he saw the hill—Vates's home— with the door. Landon stepped feebly toward it, grateful for the strong wooden stick to support him. His legs were still beneath him, trembling as they were. And then he noticed her. Gazing out at him through the window was Ditty.

Chapter Ten

Landon opened the door, stepped inside, and leaned the walking stick in the corner.

"I was praying for you," said Ditty, a look of sad relief on her face. "You had to come out on your own this time. I couldn't tap or snap you out of it. Not from Malus Quidam. Of course"—her smile now became happy—"you weren't alone, were you?"

The shadows were gone for the moment, Landon knew, yet he felt a strong urge to change clothes or bathe or do something to wipe away their effect from his body.

"I was surrounded by them," he said, pulling out a chair. He'd never felt so much relief from sitting down. "Or by—him." He cringed and then shuddered.

"That's not what I meant," said Ditty. "I knew he was out there." She cringed as well, pronouncing *he* as quietly as possible.

"No," said Landon. "I know what you meant. And

well. . .I know." He smiled. "The Auctor was there. And. . ." Landon paused. The thought of the Auctor—the Creator of the story of life—being with him out in the dark forest was a little disconcerting. It was overwhelming, actually. Landon shuddered all over again. This time he wasn't shuddering in horror or disgust. He was shaking as one so small aware of the nearness of Another so big.

"Yes," said Ditty simply. "Did you say some of his words?"

Landon nodded slowly and deeply.

Ditty's eyes glistened. "That's what I was asking, that you would remember them. When His words are spoken from the heart, He is there." She looked about the room—or at the air—and Landon knew she was basking in the Auctor's awesome presence. How could she be so calm with Him there? Landon was still shivering although his insides felt nice and warm.

Ditty sighed and looked at Landon.

"What?" said Landon, growing uneasy under her curious stare.

"That's what prophets do. They speak the Auctor's words in the face of adversity. In the face of the enemy."

Ditty came over and sat down across from him at the table. The *Book of Illumination* was open. A pointed stick, a crude sort of pencil, lay near it on the table.

"You sound more like him now," said Landon.

Ditty frowned.

"More like Vates," said Landon, and Ditty relaxed and smiled. "Like a prophet, I guess. Or a prophetess." They both laughed. "And you're reading"—Landon pointed at the book—"a lot." He leaned over the table. "And you're underlining. Now that reminds me of somebody else."

Ditty's eyes pleasantly widened. "You underline your book, too?"

Landon laughed, "I don't have to. I mean, someone else has already underlined parts for me. His name was Bartholomew G. Benneford. It's a long story." Landon glanced around. "Where is everyone? Vates, Hardy, Melech?"

"They're in the back room, planning and preparing."

"Oh," Landon said, though he had no idea what that could mean. He'd gone through enough outside with the shadows to busy his brain for now. He'd rather sit with Ditty than work on plans or preparations. Landon glanced up at two lanterns hanging overhead from a rafter. From where he sat, he couldn't see the light sources, though he guessed what was inside.

He pointed up. "Do those have fireflies in them? I mean, those, uh, firefly balls?"

Ditty looked up. "Yes." She sighed. "They're the only creatures that survived the First Descent."

"The first what?"

"That's what Vates calls it: the First Descent. Of course no one talks about it around the green."

"Echoing Green?"

Ditty nodded. "There, well, it's like it never happened. Everything changed. It was terrible. I think Ludo thinks I was too young to remember. But I do. It's when the shadows descended. Darkness fell. The strange thing is, Ludo had been the biggest animal lover of anyone. I mean, I remember!" She laughed, and her face brightened, but only briefly. Then her shoulders fell with a sigh. "I remember, Landon!"

She turned to face him, and it was almost more than

Landon could bear. No tears streamed down her cheeks, but the anguish was there. He wanted desperately to look away, but he had to hold her gaze. It was like holding her hand or hugging her, except it hurt.

"My uncle had a horse like Melech but much smaller. And chickens and cats and turtles and. . .and. . ."

Landon didn't know whether she was about to burst out sobbing or laughing. Thankfully, she did neither.

"And a funny little weasel-type thing. I don't know how I remember all this. Its name was Feister, and it poked its nose in my ear, I think. I mean, I've had dreams and woken up giggling from that sniffling tickling in my ear."

"A ferret?" Landon asked. He had a friend at school who had one, though its name was Stinky.

Ditty stared right through him. She suddenly slapped the table. Landon jumped. "A ferret! Feister the ferret!"

"But if Ludo liked animals," said Landon, "then why—"

"Everything went backwards." Ditty's eyes became piercing. "My uncle did love animals, and he was shy around people. But after he was seduced, as Vates says, he hated animals, and he started bossing people around. We weren't Odds then. We were just people or valley folk. Ludo changed physically, too. He got thinner and, well, pointier. He would point at everyone and call them odd. Eventually we all became Odds."

"So all the animals. . . ," Landon began, but he was afraid to ask. He remembered the Odds trying to take Melech away, and he cringed at the thought.

"Well, they disappeared, that's for sure." Ditty sighed. "But I don't think they were killed. My theory is he couldn't do it. There's still something good inside my uncle Ludo. He drove them all away, but he couldn't actually destroy them."

"And the fireflies?" Landon looked up. He was tempted to stand on the table and take a peek inside a lantern. "What happened to them?"

Ditty frowned for a moment. Then her expression changed, and she looked at Landon. "What? Oh. Those!" She smiled, and her voice rose with a hint of hope. "Do you know why the fireflies are still here? Because they're creatures of light." She leaned across the table. "The shadows couldn't touch them. They could only come so close and then. . ."

Ditty made a circle with her fingers and pretended to try to squeeze them together. The circle refused to collapse.

"The poor bugs fell asleep, but they didn't die. And they still glow, obviously, but at odd times." She smiled at her use of *odd*. "It's like they know when they're inside, like these." She indicated the lanterns above them. "But strangely, the ones outside—at least on Ludo's tree—only glow in the daytime. I don't know why. Anyway, since they all fell asleep and could no longer fly, they were left behind. Lucky for us, since the candle makers and wick winders had quit their jobs."

Landon thought about the forest teeming with life. For a moment it became so vivid and vibrant in his mind that he wondered if it might be true. Then the image faded. Could it have been a vision of the past? Or—and here Landon's heart fluttered with excitement—a glimpse into the future?

As Landon came back to the present, he thought of what Ditty had last said. "Candlemakers and wick winders? What are those?"

"Landon, there was a time when there was no Coin. As I

said, Ludo tended his animals. The other Odds—the valley folk—all had jobs. I mean, everyone worked because that's what they wanted to do. Everyone contributed, and everyone shared. Some made candles, some lanterns, some furniture; some cooked; some made clothes; some made stoneware, others glassware—oh, people did everything. And you know what the greatest thing of all was?"

Landon shook his head.

"The best part was that everyone gathered in and around the giant evergreen at night. It wasn't Ludo's tree. There were balconies all the way up. You could go anywhere. Evening feasts were served in the trunk. Remember when we were inside it that night?"

Landon nodded and began drifting into the memory.

Ditty stared at him. "Oh," Landon said, returning from his reverie. "Yeah, I remember. That's the night I met you." He'd said it before he could stop himself. A tingly wave climbed from his neck and warmed his face.

"Yes," said Ditty. "That's where the nightly celebrations were held. And another best part of the best part was everyone sang and danced. A lot of people played instruments. I'd nearly forgotten that part."

They remained quiet for some time. Outside it had grown completely dark. Landon noticed his and Ditty's reflection in the window.

Landon sighed. "Well, should we go join them?"

Ditty raised her eyebrows. "Who?"

"The planners and preparers," Landon said with a little laugh. "In the back room."

"All right," she said standing. "Let's go plan."

The back room was not what Landon had expected. He was picturing some sort of war room like he'd seen in a movie, with a large map on the wall and glowing computer screens and another map—or three-dimensional setup—on a vast table with little buildings and tanks and army men on it. What he saw instead was an earthen room (they were inside a hill, of course) in the middle of which stood a small table with a chessboard on it.

Besides two chairs on either side of the chess table, a wooden chaise lounge sat near a wall with a blanket on it. Vates lay reclined with a book facedown on his chest, his hands resting on the book. At first Landon thought the old man was meditating with his eyes closed, deeply pondering a plan. But then Landon heard him snoring.

Amazingly, he could hear a snoring echo that was even louder than Vates's coming from one of two narrow, open doorways. Except it wasn't an echo, Landon realized. It was Hardy.

"I thought you said they were planning and preparing," said Landon.

"They were," Ditty said, "a while ago. Hmm. Looks like Melech won again." She was looking at the chessboard, where two dark knights had the light king pinned in a corner.

Landon laughed, and Vates slowly roused.

"Yes, yes, tea and crumplets." Vates pressed the book to his chest and sat up, somewhat stiffly. He looked at Landon and blinked. He cleared his throat. "Good morning. Well, what time is it? It's later, isn't it? Evening, then. You made it, Landon Snow." He smiled. "Good. We need you. We've been waiting."

"Yeah, I see that," said Landon. "What happened out there—outside, I mean? Was that him? Malus Quidam?"

Vates sighed. "Those were his shadows. Though you saw

more of them, I daresay, than I. And you saw them more deeply. Which is for now, I think, a good thing."

Landon frowned. He pulled out a chair and sat down, and Ditty did the same. "It's a good thing?" asked Landon. "I don't want to see them anymore. They're not good things."

"It's better to know they're there and resist, as you have done, than not to recognize their presence and succumb to their influence, as many others have."

Landon fingered a rook and slid it back and forth between two squares. "So what are we planning, exactly?"

Vates swung his legs around and leaned forward, an excited glimmer in his eye. "Hardy! Melech!" he called. "It's time. Landon is here, thank the Auctor, and I believe he is ready."

A few moments later, after some groaning and yawning, Hardy and Melech stepped out from each of the doorways. Landon couldn't see much through the doorways, but there appeared to be a set of bunks in one and a short stubby stool amid a sprinkling of hay in the other. They both seemed more like stalls in a barn than rooms in a house.

Hardy blinked, stretched, yawned, gaped at Landon and Ditty as if he'd never seen them before, and then sauntered into Melech's stall to retrieve the stool. Noisily, he dragged it out and sat down, Landon's eyelids drooping.

The room was quiet save for some soft gusts from Melech's nose. Perhaps because Hardy still seemed half asleep, the atmosphere seemed more restful and relaxed than restless or anxious. Still, Landon's insides were churning with curiosity. "What am I ready for?" he asked.

"To rescue your sister, set Ludo and the valley folk free, and attack Malus Quidam," Vates said, and he smiled.

Chapter Eleven

I don't know how to plan all this," said Landon, his heart sinking. He felt as if he were letting them all down. But what was he supposed to do? He was only an eleven-year-old boy. *Just a boy,* he thought. *Sigh.*

"Well," said Vates, "perhaps we should sleep on it." He yawned and leaned back on the lounge chair. "The mind requires rest as much as the body." He turned his head and winked at Landon. "And solutions sometimes present themselves when we're least looking for them." He placed his hands behind his head, closed his eyes, smacked his lips a couple of times, and let out a prolonged exhale.

Hardy stood, his eyes still at half-mast, and shuffled past Landon mumbling, "Bedtime snack. Food for prep—" And then he broke into a yawn.

Ditty got up and followed Hardy out. Landon sat thinking about rescuing Holly and setting the Odds—the valley folk—free. Did he even want to set Ludo free, whatever that meant? And an attack on Malus Quidam? He didn't think he would be able to rest his mind by sleeping tonight.

Without thinking, Landon brushed the table and set a few chess pieces wobbling. The cornered king teetered and then vibrated to a standstill. Vates let out a soft, sighing snore. How could he be so calm? Melech appeared calm, as well. He was looking at Landon.

Landon smiled at Melech and then gestured toward the table. "So you play chess now on a small board like this?"

Melech gently snorted. "Hardy moves the pieces. I only tell him where to place them."

"And together you two beat Vates?" He glanced at the snoring prophet.

"We did, yes."

"With two knights?" Landon raised his eyebrows at Melech.

Melech bared his teeth in a gleeful grin. "No one moves quite like a knight you know, young Landon."

Landon laughed. "I do know, after that bumpy ride on the board with you last year." That seemed so long ago now. Landon lightly tapped the corner of the board near the trapped king. "And it looks like no one *thinks* quite like a knight, either. You know, you'd be good to help plan this attack, Melech. Will you help me?"

"Young Landon, I will do my duty and be glad for it."

"A noble deed for a noble steed."

Melech pricked his ears but remained silent.

Ditty returned with two mugs. She set one on each side of the table. "What's going on?" She glanced between Landon and Melech.

"Oh, we're remembering old times," said Landon. "And planning future ones." He took a few sips of what he thought would be ginger ale. He was relieved to find it was water. He'd needed that. Landon set down the mug, took a deep breath, and closed his eyes. When he opened them, Ditty was watching him.

"I can't believe all this is happening," Landon said. "And that Vates wants me to plan the attack. I like to figure things out, but I've never tried anything like this. Not even close." Landon closed his eyes and sighed.

"We're all here to help," Ditty said. "And we're not alone."

Landon nodded and opened his eyes. "Yes. With the Auctor's help, we can do this, I suppose. It's just, well, we'll need a lot of help."

"We'll ask for a lot then." Ditty smiled and then bowed her head and closed her eyes.

"Ditty?" Landon said tentatively, sorry to interrupt her. She glanced up. "Could you ask for help for Holly, too? I'm a little scared for her. And I feel like it's my fault for, for. . ."

Ditty's eyes widened with compassion, and Landon felt a lump jam his throat like a fist. *Don't cry,* he told himself, sensing twin puddles forming beneath his eyes. He blinked fiercely and cleared his throat.

"Holly wouldn't be here if it wasn't for me," he said finally. "I told her about you and about Hardy and Vates and this place and that I wanted to come back here." Landon sighed. "As much as I wanted to come back here, I wanted to bring her with me to. . .to prove this to her."

"To prove what?"

Landon gazed at her. "That you're real. That this is real.

And that it really happened."

"So you got your wish." Ditty tilted her head.

"Yeah. I guess. Although I never expected it to turn out like this."

The room was quiet. Landon stared unseeing at the chess game.

"Landon?"

He looked at her.

"I'll ask for help for her, too. And for you."

A small smile pushed at his cheeks. "Thanks."

Ditty closed her eyes and lowered her head. After watching her a moment, Landon slowly and quietly stood. He suddenly felt he needed something to hold on to. Something firm and stable. He thought of getting Vates's staff to simply lean on for strength. As he took a step, he reached out and pressed Melech's neck.

He stopped and held it. Melech's velvety dark hide twitched and then lay still. Landon held his hand there. This was better than a knobby, wood staff. Landon could feel the cords of Melech's powerful neck muscles. He combed his fingers through the coarse mane. With the touch of Melech's body and the quiet prayers of Ditty for help, Landon was feeling much better. He looked at Melech and whispered, "I think I might be able to sleep now. Thanks, Melech." He patted his neck one more time.

"Of course, young Landon," Melech said quietly. "Sleep thee well."

After three more sips of water, Landon nodded good night to Ditty and Melech and then headed for the small room on the left with the bunks. The bottom bunk looked neat and tidy, not like Hardy could have used it. Landon climbed in, lay back, and rested.

When a noise woke him, Landon realized he had fallen asleep. Hardy was clambering into the top bunk. Almost immediately, a wheezy whistling started. Hardy's snoring became the whistling of a bird.

"Twee-too! Twee-too!" It was the only sound in an otherwise empty forest. Landon knew it was a special bird, and he set off after it, nearly flying himself.

The bird's call led Landon to a giant pine tree that he recognized as Ludo's tree. Then something frightening and marvelous happened. The bird fluttered overhead, though it flew too quickly for Landon to see it very well. It came swooping up behind him, and the next thing Landon knew— he was flying. Up and up he rose, right to the balcony with the dangling lenses. Yet he didn't land on the balcony. He continued flying through the doorway and down the corridor inside the giant branch. He was flying inside the tree, and he realized with some astonishment that he was the bird. But he seemed even smaller—as if he'd shrunk right down to the size of a fly.

So Landon flew to a hallway and then up some steps to another branch corridor and another balcony. He heard a voice outside that he recognized. Holly. She was saying numbers: "205, 206, 207, 208." She was counting, of course. If not overly excited (how excited can a person be, counting?), she at least sounded content.

Landon alighted on a wall, hoping he wouldn't be swatted. He could see her now. She was using a crude pencil to jot down marks on a piece of wood. And she was actually—Landon noticed with some alarm—not standing on the deck but being hoisted in a leather seat. Ropes ran up and down from her leather harness, and Landon imagined a pulley system that was lifting her through the tree. Kind of like what a rock climber would use, although this looked much more primitive.

Landon decided to see how she was doing.

Flying close to her shoulder but just out of swat range (in case he was buzzing; he couldn't tell), Landon said, "Holly, it's me. Are you okay?"

Ignoring him, she said, "231, 232, 233."

He flew in closer. She was wearing coveralls like the Odds wore. "Holly? Can you hear me?"

She paused, making another mark on the wood. They weren't simple hash marks, Landon noted with surprise, but complex figures and designs. What on earth was she writing? He was about to speak again when she seemed to look right at him, her eyes crossing slightly. "Landon? What are you doing here?"

For some reason, the question threw him. A moment later, however, he said, "I was worried about you."

Holly smiled. With her eyes still crossed, this did not make the most assuring of expressions. "Worried? But I'm having fun. I'm counting."

"Yes. I can see that. Ludo's not harming you?"

She blinked and frowned. "Harm? No, I'm fine. They call me Second-to-None!"

Landon felt like he'd been swatted away. Actually he'd only done a backflip on his own. "What? You? But. . .but. . ." He felt like spitting. "I was Second-to-None. That's what they called me. There can't be two of us."

Holly turned away and pointed to something in the tree, saying, "242, 243."

Landon felt his own eyes crossing in anger. "That Ludo! I hate him. He can't do this to me. Making my own sister Second-to-None. There can only be one of us."

Holly glanced up from scratching on her little board. "Hmm? Did you say something?"

Landon tried to breathe. This was turning into a nightmare. Then he thought, *Hey, this really is turning into a nightmare. I can't fly like this, like a bird or a bug, in real life. I'm dreaming! And maybe this dream is trying to tell me something.*

A rickety rolling noise startled him. Holly was going up. Landon followed, climbing on air.

"You're still here?" said Holly. "Can't you see I'm busy?"

"So you're Second-to-None," said Landon. He wanted to probe, but he wasn't sure for what. "Why did they call you that? Did you pass some sort of test? When I was here, I'd told them Maple Tree Max had fired over ninety arrows at me." He laughed, remembering the moment with a touch of pride. "The truth was—"

"I'm really busy, Landon. Can't you see how busy I am? Perhaps you should buzz off. Now where was I? Ah, 567, 568, 569."

Landon wanted to swat his sister away for being so rude. Maybe he could at least land on her ear and give her an annoying sting or bite. Flying in, he feared getting caught and tangled in her hair. So he hung back.

"Hey," said Landon, "weren't you just in the two hundreds down there? Why'd you skip so many numbers?"

An exasperated sigh preceded the turning of her head. Landon backed out of reach. "If you must know, I'm working out calculations. See?" She raised the wooden board and withdrew it again. The symbols and numbers came and went in a blur. "I'm not just counting them. That's kids' stuff. I'm figuring out their population density by altitude."

Landon felt himself frowning. What was she talking about?

"Of course, the numbers get smaller the higher we go. We could look at each branch as a radius. The branches get shorter, so the circumference decreases accordingly. Less circumference, less area for the population."

"The population?" said Landon, feeling thoroughly confused. Could he really be dreaming this stuff? And if so, why? "What population?"

Suddenly, a glare so bright vanquished everything from sight. Gradually the glowing broke apart into thousands of dots of light. They were like stars, except between them lay not darkness but light. The dots remained while between them the light slowly dimmed until Landon could see the color green. Then the lights themselves spread farther apart, and he found he was looking into the branches among the long green needles of Ludo's tree. Where was Holly?

"One million!"

Landon looked up. There she was, somehow dangling at the very top of the tree.

"Of course, that's a conservative estimate," she mumbled as Landon zipped up to her level. "And look at this. At the highest point—which is only a point with no radius or area—we have a population of one."

Landon was able to drift comfortably near her elbow in the open air. And he saw what she was writing—or what she had written—on the little board clearly for the first time. Whereas before it had appeared a bunch of messy gibberish, now it appeared a simple, if yet still unclear, diagram.

At the top was a circle with a slightly rough edge and a fancy sun drawn in its center. Landon was sure it must be the Coin. Below it was a half circle, round side up, with what appeared to be tiny trees on either side of it. And then at the bottom were a lot of odd shapes that seemed to be pieces of a puzzle. No one piece matched any other, yet they somehow seemed as if they might all fit together.

A hand covered the pictures. "Hey! What are you looking at?"

Landon tumbled back through the air. Holly was glaring at him fiercely, when suddenly her expression changed. She lifted her hand and pointed directly at him. "One million and one," she said. "And how come you're not in the tree? And how"—she paused and glanced down, then looked back at Landon—"how are you doing that? None of the others can fly. How come you can?"

"What are you talking about?" Landon began to say. His sister wouldn't have heard him, though. She had reached out to grab him, and her hand grew into a dark mass that blotted everything out. Unable to fly away, Landon tensed, prepared to be cupped or crushed in her hand. A call burst the air, and something began to pluck the darkness away, strip by strip. It was the familiar two-note song of that bird. What was its name?

As the dream world started to fade, Landon heard his sister's voice echoing down a long tunnel. "You're glowing, Landon. You can glow. . . ."

Landon imagined himself falling through the air and being gathered upon the wings of the calling bird in midflight. Upward they swooped and then downward again, racing back through the wood in time for—

Opening his eyes, Landon heard a sound that was real. And it wasn't Hardy snoring. A bird was singing a two-note song over and over.

"Epops," Landon said rousing. His dream floated in his mind like rags in a whirlwind.

"Twee-too! Twee-too!"

The call was sharp and crisp. Epops was in the house!

Landon could see the planning room. The chess table and the chairs were dim shapes in the weak light. A large figure suddenly loomed within the doorframe, and Landon sat up and bumped his head on the sagging bottom of the upper bunk. Above him, a muffled cry came in response.

"I hope you two found some rest." It was Vates's voice. "The shadows are swarming. If we are to attack, the time is now."

Chapter Twelve

The top bunk let out a moan as the lump near Landon's head rolled toward the wall.

"What time is it?" asked Landon. He was blinking his eyes, trying to see better.

"It's early morning yet, but well after sunrise."

Landon couldn't believe it. It felt like it was the dead of the night. "It's so dark," he said in a hushed voice.

"And getting darker, I'm afraid." Vates produced a lantern and set it on a small table. Reaching in, he flicked at something with his finger. A small light began to glow. "Wake up, lightning bug," the old man said. "Even they're having difficulty fighting this darkness." A couple more flicks, and the firefly glowed brighter, though beyond its yellow halo, dingy shadows still clung to the room.

Excitedly, Landon leaned over to see if the firefly had awakened. But no, it looked as lifeless as ever, despite the faintly pulsing light from its abdomen. "Poor bug."

Vates remained in the doorway. "I hope you had an interesting dream or two."

The light seemed to flicker like a candle flame struggling against a draft. Vates's face and hair seemed transformed into a mane of snow around craggy rock, his eyes glistening as two exotic jewels. For a moment Landon wondered if he might still be dreaming.

"I saw my sister," he said. "She was counting fireflies in Ludo's tree."

"Hmm." Vates seemed to be waiting for more.

"She was writing things down, too. Strange notations at first. But then three things." The images were returning. "The Coin, I think. And a half circle—well, something like a big round tent maybe among some trees. And some funny shapes that looked like a puzzle."

Vates was nodding, muttering, "Good, good. Very good. You have received a vision, young man. And this old man has dreamed a dream. Now we must make haste, and we'll talk along the way. You there!" Vates stepped in and poked over Landon's head with his stick. "You'll meet us at the Stepping Stone by noon. You can't count on the sun for the time; it won't be seen much today. So up, Hardy, up!"

Another jab elicited a grunt and a muffled cry of complaint. The bunk creaked, and two feet appeared almost atop Landon's head. He glanced up, crinkled his nose, and ducked out from under them.

Vates retreated from the doorway, and Landon heard his voice trailing as he left the next room. "It is time to make haste. Landon, gather your things"—Vates paused and turned back—"uh, well, get your sister's coat. I guess that's about all you brought." He flashed a brief smile, though it was difficult to see it in the semidarkness. "And come with me. Ditty, you, and I will ride Melech. He's already out front." He disappeared.

Landon stood still and quiet for a moment. He could make out the light and dark squares of the chessboard. They were hardly black and white in this muted light. A shiver ran up his spine as he thought what they were about to do. *We're going to attack a bunch of shadows*, he thought. And how exactly does one do that? He could resist their seductive whispers by remembering the Auctor's presence and speaking His words. But to *attack* them? This seemed futile.

Hardy stepped out, grumbling as he pulled up the straps of his coveralls. Landon turned and said, "How are you going to meet us there without Melech?" He felt badly that Hardy wouldn't ride with them.

Stretching and moaning, Hardy grinned and said, "Before horsy show up, I make trip all de time. Quick and nimble."

Appraising the stout figure before him, Landon wanted to laugh. Despite his big grin, however, Hardy seemed quite sincere.

"Well." Hardy patted his belly. "Before getting lazy and fat!" He plopped himself down on the stool and pulled on some boots. "Breakfast, and I'll see you dere." He stood, nodded, and clomped from the room.

Taking another moment, Landon looked at the ceiling. "We could really use some help," he said, hoping his plea was heard. "And please protect Holly."

With that, he headed to the front room, which was hardly any lighter. Ditty sat at the table, but her book wasn't there.

She wore a bulky pack on her back, and Landon guessed the book was inside. This made him feel better. Silently, she directed him to what looked like thick stale bread stacked on a tin platter. Beside the platter was a mug, which Landon eagerly put to his lips. The ginger juice fizzed and burned and warmed his insides. It didn't taste too bad, either. The hard bread, however, did not look very appetizing.

Ditty spoke. "Eat. You'll feel better. And you'll need the energy."

Landon looked at her, amazed. She seemed to have grown up so much since he'd first met her. Had he grown up some, too?

Reluctantly he took a piece of bread and bit into it. It crunched between his teeth, and he started to grimace, prepared to spit it out. The more he chewed, however, the softer it became. And when he swallowed, it went down easily, and he immediately took another bite. "You're right," he said with a nod. "I feel better already."

Ditty smiled and motioned toward the door. "They're waiting outside, and Hardy's already gone. He bet me an apple he'd get to the stone first. Let's go."

"Mmnph," Landon said, gnawing and quickly gulping. He touched Ditty's elbow as she turned. When their gazes met, he said, "I asked for help."

She held his gaze for a moment. "Me, too. We're going to need it."

The scene outside Vates's hill was strange. At first it appeared to be snowing—except the flakes weren't white. They were black. Was dirt falling from the sky? Had there been an explosion somewhere, sending up bits of soil that now came—strangely and slowly—dropping back to earth? When the black specks touched the ground, they connected with others near them. And when enough had chained together, the resulting dark line meshed with other lines until a figure had formed that was wide as a snake. Then the shadow would silently wriggle away to the woods.

"Hurry!" Vates said, and Ditty and Landon clambered to mount Melech. Vates's voice grew husky, making him sound even more ancient than his years. "Malus Quidam is gathering his shadows. I've never seen so much darkness in one place. This is truly the Second Descent."

Landon swallowed his last bite of hard bread. He had another slice along, but he'd had his fill for now and wasn't so hungry. He was glad he'd started eating before coming out to witness. . .this.

Melech set off at a trot. Although they seemed intent on hurrying, he did not break into a full-out gallop. They were going fast enough to avoid falling shadows—some of which came down the size of blankets—but at a pace hedged with some caution. It seemed they were possibly on the lookout for something, although Landon knew not what.

Landon thought about his dream, which now seemed like so much faraway nonsense. What did it have to do with anything? Were they still hoping that he would come up with some sort of a plan? Before they reached the river, and by all means before arriving at the Echoing Green, he thought he'd better ask. First, he thought he'd start with a seemingly simpler query.

"Why aren't we going any faster? I thought we had to hurry."

Vates seemed almost startled, as if he'd completely forgotten Landon was seated behind him. (Vates held the reins up front, while Ditty sat in the middle, and Landon was in back. He was grateful her leather pack was so convenient to hold on to, as the idea of clasping her midsection made him feel a bit dizzy and faint.)

"Ditty is directing me," Vates said over his shoulder. "Though you may not be able to see it, she's tapping me to go left or right. As the shadows thicken, the true path becomes more difficult to see. She holds the *Book of Illumination*, which is our true guide. Oh!" Vates jerked the reins to the right, and Landon swayed abruptly.

"The book illumines our path," Ditty murmured, apparently concentrating on the hazy trees—or shadows that looked like trees—ahead.

Landon squeezed the pack. If the book was packed away, how could it guide them? He was about to ask about this when he thought of how much he'd seen her reading it. If he could remember passages from his Bible from his reading the past five months, he wondered how much of the *Book of Illumination* Ditty might have memorized in that time. *Besides,* he thought, *time seems to travel more quickly here than back in my world.*

"Here comes the river," Ditty said. Landon felt the pack rise and fall as she shrugged and pointed.

"Well done, Ditty," Vates said. "Very well done. We will rest here a spell, now that we've made it this far. "This kind of work is more taxing than mere physical exertion. And Landon, you and I have some dreams to discuss. Hmm?"

A loud splash startled them. Then another splash sounded

from the river, followed by a raucous but friendly laugh.

"Ha ha! An apple for me! An apple for me! An apple for me. . ."

More splashes were heard as Hardy's voice faded across the water. One last shout made it clearly back. "See you on de odder side, Ditty!" After a faint, softer splash, no more noises came from the direction of the river.

"Must have run out of stones again," said Ditty. Her voice sounded almost playful, as if she were teasing Hardy from afar.

"Lily Pad Crossing," Landon said wistfully. He imagined the stone circles forming in the shape of giant lily pads and then shrinking until they disappeared. Suddenly he thought of something and leaned around Ditty's shoulder.

"If we had to be so careful, how come Hardy can just run through the forest?"

Vates appeared to lift his head at the question. "There is nothing like simple innocence to open one's way." He swung sideways to see Landon. "Hardy has his faults, too. But if pride is a hook upon which the shadows hang themselves and tug, well, Hardy's hook is more like a flattened nail. There's just not much there to yank on."

"How about you?" Landon said. "Vates, you're the smartest and wisest person I know."

Vates looked out at the river for a long time. The water was visible in gray patches here and there between the shifting black shadows. It almost appeared that a black tarpaulin had been draped across the river and then had been attacked by piranhas. Finally, Vates turned back to Landon.

"Exactly," said Vates slowly. "Why do you think I live so far away?"

Landon was stunned. "You were tempted, too? To take over from Ludo and lead them?"

"That and so much more," Vates said wearily. "Though today we are hurrying, my time has mostly been spent waiting. And waiting, Landon Snow—especially when one knows so much and even thinks he wants to do good—is perhaps the hardest thing to do."

"I didn't want to wait to go back for Holly."

"Yet you made it another day. And now the time is ripening."

Vates and Landon dismounted and found a dry, sandy area on which to sit. Vates took out his special lantern with the directional beam, the one he'd used to rid all the "leech" shadows from Landon's back. Making a half-circle sweep one way, and then the other, Vates cleared the immediate area of slinking shadows. Ditty had stepped into the tall grass and was gathering stones for the river crossing in a bag, which she had just produced from her pack.

"Now about our dreams. . ."

Vates pulled out a rolled parchment and spread it open on the ground. It was blank. Next, Vates took out a strange-looking writing utensil that had its own built-in inkwell. The sight of Vates with pen and parchment made Landon think of the Auctor's Riddle. He mouthed it silently to himself:

Could it be chance, mere circumstance
That man eats cow eats grass eats soil
And then man dies, and when he lies
To soil he does return?

Could it be chance, coincidence?
That sun turns earth turns moon turns seas
And so there are years, and salty beach tears
So ticks celestial time

Or might there be one above creation
Who designed and created and shaped and colored
Who put where they are, the earth, moon, and star
And a boy named Landon Snow to wonder. . .in awe.

"The dreams," Vates was saying. "Our dreams, Landon, may hold the key to setting the valley people free."

The black bits of shadow continued to fall. Interestingly, they floated away from where Vates and Landon were sitting, as if an invisible umbrella were shielding them. Or rather, Landon noticed, it seemed the shadows were drawn to other shadows. So as they neared the earth, they veered toward other already dark patches as if being pulled by a black hole.

Urgency returned to Vates's demeanor as he leaned forward and spoke, his writing pen at the ready. "You mentioned three images that Holly had drawn in your dream. What were they?"

Landon thought hard. "The first was the Coin, I'm pretty sure."

Vates nodded and drew a circle. "Second?"

"Mm. It was a half circle surrounded by trees. Like it was on the ground."

Vates looked up but not at Landon. He appeared to be thinking. "A dome, perhaps?"

Landon frowned and thought about it. Gradually, he

nodded. "Yeah, I guess it was like a dome—a dome in the forest?"

Vates drew a dome shape with a tree on either side. "Interesting," he muttered. "Next?"

"Well, there were a bunch of funny shapes but not together. I think they looked like they might fit together, like a puzzle. I'm not sure why they seemed like that, though."

Vates drew three shapes that appeared to be part of a larger whole. "And now I will tell you what I saw. First"—he began to draw wavy lines next to the Coin—"there was fire. Yes, that's fire." He tapped the squiggly lines.

"Next, I saw tools, specifically the tools of the valley folk." Beside the tree-bordered dome, he sketched some rudimentary instruments. Landon recognized a mallet or hammer, a spike or chisel, and something that might be a drill, though he couldn't be sure.

"Finally, to go with your mysterious puzzle pieces, we have, well. . ." Vates struggled to get something down. Landon squinted and frowned.

"Is that a tree?" asked Landon.

"Yes. Actually the inside of a tree—Ludo's tree. Inside the trunk."

"Where he has all your old signs from the woods?" Landon recalled the stacks of tables and chairs, as well as the dusty bar and cobweb-covered cabinets.

"Apparently so, yes. Now these first two, I think I may understand. Yes, I really do. But this last one, I'm not so sure of at all. Hmm. Somehow I get the feeling we needn't quite worry about the last part yet, anyway. What we must do is get started at the top." He sighed. "Yes, this will be tricky.

So, do you see what I see?"

Landon studied the drawings. He wished there was better light. It was like trying to read something by starlight. It was strange having shadows falling all over the place.

"This first one. . .the Coin is to be melted by fire?" He glanced at Vates, and the old prophet's eyes were gleaming. Encouraged, Landon looked at the next pair of sketches. "And we're supposed to put up a tent—"

Vates's expression dropped, so Landon tried again. He looked at the simple tools, then at the fire above them. *If the Coin were melted and then cooled. . .*

"The Coin is to be crafted, uh, hammered into a big dome?"

The gleam returned to Vates's eyes. Figuring out the clues was fun for Landon.

"And this"—Landon circled the dome between the trees—"is the Echoing Green." He spoke with confidence. "I see something else now. It wasn't in Holly's sketch in my dream. But I'm seeing it now. . .something all over the dome."

Vates placed the pen tip near the dome, awaiting further instruction.

"May I?" said Landon.

Handing Landon the pen, Vates smiled and sat up. "Draw away, Landon Snow."

"I'm a terrible artist," said Landon. "Although all I see is, well. . .this." Sticking out his tongue in concentration, he proceeded to draw tiny circles all over the dome. When he was done, he sat back and held it up. "It looks like a giant ladybug," he said. "With very small spots." Landon shook his head and shrugged his shoulders. "Whatever that means."

"Indeed," said Vates, staring in amazement at the ladybug. "You're on the right track, Landon. Not a ladybug, but. . ."

Landon blinked. In a flash the scene from his dream returned. "She was counting fireflies in the tree. And then she counted me. I think I was a firefly, too, in my dream." His heart began to pound. Pointing at the dots, he said excitedly, "Not a ladybug, but a dome of fireflies! A place where shadows can't hide—"

Landon cut himself short with a gasp. "It's the trap!"

Around them the shadows froze as if everything had been put on pause. When the shadows resumed moving, they fell faster than seemed possible. No longer were they drifting as dark flakes or feathers. Now they began to zoom toward earth, and once collected on the ground, the larger swaths of shadows began to glide toward the river and across it.

"It's like they heard us," Landon said quietly. His stomach was twisting into a knot. "What are we going to do?"

"The question isn't what, but how. You just explained what needs to be done." Vates tapped the parchment. "And I'm very curious to see how it happens." With that Vates rolled up the paper, rose, and tucked it somewhere inside his robe. "Time to hurry again."

Landon got up quickly to stay close to Vates. They strode to Melech. Ditty was there, her book open on her lap. The book appeared to be glowing, and Landon thought of its title. The *Book of Illumination* indeed! Landon's excitement fell when he saw Ditty lift the real source of the light from the pages. It was a firefly ball. Ditty closed the book and stuffed it into her pack.

Vates mounted and asked Ditty if she was ready. Pointing

to a bag of stones on the ground, Vates said, "Landon, would you mind doing the honors?"

Landon picked up the bag, amazed at its weight. He glanced at Ditty's thin little hands and grimaced. Heaving the bag onto Melech's rump, Landon clambered aboard while clasping the mouth of the sack with one hand. He kept this hand pressing it behind him. "Ready," he said, hoping he was up to the task.

"Here." Ditty offered him two ends of a belt, which he saw already went around her waist. "Forgot I had it. Brought it for this part of the trip anyway, so you won't fall off."

"I could always take you with me," Landon said with a grin. Ditty made a face, and Landon's cheeks went hot. "Sorry. Thanks." Trusting the sack to balance for a few seconds, Landon let it go to use both his hands to fasten the belt around him. He regrabbed the sack and exhaled. "Ready," he said again.

Melech turned his head. "Ditty? Straight ahead?"

"Yes." Ditty nodded. "The river's clear enough. But the shadows will make the stone pads harder to see, so Landon? You've got to throw them perfectly straight ahead."

Great, Landon thought. *More pressure.* His stomach untwisted and then retied the other way. A jolt signaled it was time to grab the first stone. They were bounding down the bank toward the water. The dark expanse before him caused Landon to freeze up.

"Throw, Landon!" Ditty cried. "Throw!"

At the last instant, his arm loosened, and he fished open the sack. With only the leather belt holding him to Ditty, Landon was bouncing and swaying like a rag doll. *Straight ahead,* he told himself. *Straight ahead!* He felt something hard and cool in his grasp. Landon watched the bobbing heads in front of him and then tossed the stone over them. *Splash!* A second later they were up in the air, Landon leaning back and praying for the strap to hold. Down they came, and he bounced against Ditty's sack as Melech's hoofs clattered across the first pad of stone.

Chapter Thirteen

There was no time to think as they crossed the river. It took all of Landon's concentration and strength to keep the stones flying at the right interval and in the right direction. The amazing thing was they made it with three stones to spare.

Landon was about to release the sack, glad to be rid of it. At the last moment, however, he remembered it was Ditty's and simply tucked it under his leg—after dumping out the remaining three stones. Also beneath his legs draped across Melech like an extra saddle was Holly's jacket. Landon breathed a sigh of relief that it was still here. He patted the pockets and felt the notebook, pen, calculator, and tape measure. Landon smiled at his sister's peculiarities.

Spreading his arms like wings, Landon took a moment to enjoy the freedom Ditty's belt provided. He swayed easily with Melech's brisk and steady lope. As he brought in his hands to take hold of Ditty's leather pack, she turned her head, sending a few stray hairs into his face. "Nice job," she said.

"Thanks," said Landon. "You, too."

"Well, we're not there yet." She faced forward, and Landon could sense her tapping Vates's left shoulder. Almost immediately they swerved in that direction.

Something rattled overhead. Frozen leaves clattered against each other. Landon gasped, half expecting an Odd to be peering down at them with an arrow notched and aimed. Then he exhaled with relief. What he saw was not an Odd but a little green bird. Suddenly everything seemed a little brighter.

"Epops!"

The bird flew down and alighted on Landon's shoulder, hopping down his arm and then flitting to Ditty's head, where it perched like an ornament atop a weathervane. Though the bird was small and fairly light as a clump of feathers, Landon was a little surprised that he hadn't felt its weight or clutching claws or hopping movements at all upon his arm. He tapped his arm along the path Epops had hopped. Nothing. Alarmed, Landon realized he also couldn't feel anything in his hand and fingers, which were tapping his arm. "I'm going numb," he said. "I can't feel anything."

Vates leaned to one side and craned his head. The old man's face appeared chiseled, and his eyes looked like marbles with gray-blue circles. Even his hair appeared stiff. Was it really that cold? Was everything turning to ice?

"The shadows are beginning to harden us, Landon. It's a good sign in one sense. They're not getting inside—we're not listening and letting them in to turn our hearts to rust and our minds to mold." Vates was hardly moving his mouth. It was like he was a ventriloquist. "The bad news is the closer we get to attacking them and the more we resist, the harder it gets. No pun intended." Something in his tone suggested a smile, though it wasn't at all apparent on his face.

Landon's heart beat fiercely. He felt like he was wearing a tight plastic mask when he tried to speak. "You keep saying 'attack.' I still don't understand what we're actually going to do."

"We're doing it," said Vates mysteriously, "by charging in on faith and hope."

Ditty turned her head halfway. It broke Landon's heart to see her becoming more rigid, too. "And love," she said softly.

Vates and Ditty both faced forward, and Landon was relieved not to have to look any longer at their statuelike faces. Flocks of silent bat shadows and the slithering mass of snake shadows were creepy, but Landon hadn't felt real worry or fear until now. Apparently the shadows were still whispering to him and the others, but they didn't hear them. Landon knew that real bats sent out sound waves like radar. He now understood that the shadows were speaking among themselves all around him, sending out vile messages. Those invisible waves of evil were pressing in, trying to get at his mind and his heart.

Though I walk through the valley of shadows, I will not fear. . . .

Melech seemed to be slowing. Landon tapped his hide. It felt almost like wood.

How are we supposed to attack when we can't move? Landon didn't try to get the words out. It was enough effort to simply sit and breathe and try to think. It was getting more difficult to see. When something quickly moved from behind a tree, Landon would have jumped if he could have. His stiff limbs, however, held him fast.

The figure approached, and Landon felt his heart knocking inside, wanting to escape. He was sure it was a shadow-wolf, and he could do nothing but watch and wait. So much for their "attack." He didn't think he could resist the darkness any longer.

But what was this? The wolf seemed to be walking on its hind legs. And stiffly. It was coming not in swift bounds but by waddling, or rather rocking back and forth like a rigid mummy.

"Stepping Stone," it said, panting despite its slow movement. "Hardy won. Ditty owes apple!"

Landon wanted to cry with relief, though he feared the tears might freeze on his face.

Hardy led them back to the tree, where one side was a large, tiered rock that looked almost like porch steps leading up to the trunk. Hardy climbed the steps, slowly turned, and somehow bent his knees enough to sit down. "Hardy. . .getting . . .hard," he said. "And heavy."

Landon leaned to his right and let his body fall from Melech to the ground. It barely hurt. The fact that he did feel a tiny ping in his right shoulder upon impact made him extremely happy. At least he could still feel something. His happiness was short-lived, however, as he worked to rock his body until he could roll over. Then he struggled vainly for what seemed several minutes to get up. Finally, though he didn't feel it, he noticed that his body was somehow lifting from the ground. And then he was standing.

Hardy stepped out from behind Landon. Apparently the Odd had hoisted Landon up by the armpits. Then Hardy returned to the steps and, with a great heaving groan, collapsed.

"Thanks," Landon muttered. The one word took a lot out of him. It was good he was on his feet, though. It felt easier to stand than to do anything else. He felt rather like a tree rooted in place.

Vates and Ditty had managed to dismount and get themselves seated on the ground near the stepping stone. Ditty was staring at the book in her lap, though it was closed. "Epops," she said, her voice soft and fluttery as a breeze, "help."

The bird had been hopping between them, going from shoulder to head to arm to shoulder. It had just been bouncing along Melech's back when it heard Ditty's cry, cocked its head only a moment, and swung down to her left hand. In a little dance, Epops climbed Ditty's left arm, circled her neck, and skipped down her right arm. It paused a moment, swiveling its head from the book to Ditty's face. In that moment, Landon had a vision in which he and the others—Ditty and Vates on the ground, Hardy on the steps, and he and Melech standing nearby—were all statues. Actual figures of stone in the forest, while this one little bird hopped playfully among them. Landon wished he were a birdbath clasping a bowl of water in ringed arms that Epops could come and splash and play in. In this strange yet somehow wonderful moment, Landon saw how unaffected this bird was by the shadows. It was the only truly living creature in a petrified forest, just as it had been the only animal not driven out when the shadows first descended. And as long as this bird was with them, Landon knew everything would be okay. Somehow.

Epops clutched at the book's cover, flapped his wings in a flash of green and white, and flew to Ditty's other hand. He looked back and forth between her face and the book, while Ditty seemed to be reading. At first Landon couldn't hear her. As she continued on, word by word, sentence by sentence, paragraph by paragraph, her struggling, faltering voice grew stronger. In what seemed a nod of approval, Epops bobbed a little dance, flew to Ditty's right hand, and turned another page. Ditty read about how light from above would break through the enclosing shadows, entrapping them and breaking them and scattering the darkness to the winds.

" 'And as the shadows of Malus Quidam are dispersed east of east and west of west, so the people in the valley will be set free. They will resume their trades of arts and crafts and music, the purpose for which they were placed. Light will guide their days and sprinkle their nights. And the Auctor's voice will be remembered once again.' "

As she finished and fell silent, Landon felt a chill pass over his skin, and he shuddered. It was a good shudder, however, because with it, he realized his flesh was less numb. He could feel the air! And if he could feel the air. . .

Landon squeezed his arm and felt the thickness of it beneath the crisp texture of his jacket. Yes, the jacket was a bit stiff, but that was from the cold. Landon flexed his elbow and bent his knees.

"I can move," he said. "And I can feel."

"Stranged!" Hardy shouted, and he stood on the top step

of the stone. As Landon watched Hardy stretch and bend his arms, he decided he must have said *strength*, not *stranged*. "Time to save da day!"

Vates, too, rose from the ground, and he appeared taller than ever. The sight of his face—still weathered but not craggy—filled Landon with confidence. "Not only has the reading strengthened us. . . ," said Vates, "look."

A path of light led a way through the darkness. It curved this way and that, meandering easily among the trees and shadows. Landon gasped. He thought it was the most beautiful thing he had ever seen.

"Quickly!" said Vates. "Let us follow before our eyes again grow dim and our hearts falter."

The three mounted Melech while Hardy jogged happily ahead. It was a shimmering tunnel. Landon knew the shadows were moving thickly about them, but they could not penetrate the light. Every now and then, he thought he heard a yelp nearby on either side, as a dog might cry stepping on a thorn. Gradually, the light began to fade. Or was it only Landon's worry that it might fade, that it might not guide their path forever? Whether he worried first or the light flickered first, he wasn't sure. But once he did worry, the yelps outside became louder. And they were no longer sharp whimpers but growls and snarls and even barks.

A shadow crossed their path.

Melech reared up. Landon grabbed Ditty's backpack as Vates yelled, "Whoa!" and then, "Plow on, Melech!"

Melech charged, and Landon wondered if anyone could see. He was no longer merely worried. His heart was hammering with fear. Any moment, he thought, a black wolf

would tear him from Melech's back, and he would be lost in
darkness. He tried to remember the words Ditty had read.
He tried remembering words from his own book, the Bible.
But now, worse than his body becoming numb, his mind was
freezing up. He was drawing a total blank on everything. All
he could do was hold on. One word finally came to mind,
and it was all he could do to keep thinking it over and over.
Help. Help. Help.

Melech had stopped running pell-mell through the forest
and had broken sharply right. They now seemed to be moving
along a fairly clear path. Landon, still clutching Ditty's pack
with a death grip, opened his eyes. Something was different.
They had reached a place the shadows had been trying to
keep them from. Though it still seemed darker than a starless,
moonless midnight, Landon noticed something. Trees. Real
trees of wood and branches and frozen leaves. They weren't
mere shadows. And beneath the trees, in a link of continuous
bodies—all rather short although their height fluctuated
one to the next—ran a line of people. The line continued
in a long, sweeping curve on Landon's right. To his left
was. . .nothing. It was a big open space. And Landon realized
where he was.

Chapter Fourteen

They haven't come out yet," Vates said to Hardy. "You must join them tonight to tow the Coin onto the field. Take these." Vates handed Hardy two objects. "And when you strike, strike hard, fast, and true. We'll want a bonfire tonight on the green. Wait for Landon's signal."

Hardy shoved the objects into his coveralls and scurried off.

Wait for my signal? Landon thought. *What signal?* "What was that about?" he asked.

"That was phase one," said Vates, leaning out and craning his neck to look back. "Though I'm still not sure what phase two is."

"What did you give him?"

"A piece of scrapestone and a steel chisel. When scrapestone chips, it sparks."

Landon still didn't understand, though he had a strange feeling this was actually making some sort of sense. "And what's my signal?" he said.

After a pause, Vates said, "I guess we'll just have to see when we see, won't we?"

As Landon mulled this over, Ditty spoke quietly. "Is she up there, you think?"

Landon knew whom she meant and what she meant. The thought sickened him, and a dull ache nibbled at his heart. He began to quaver with doubt and fear, but a faint speck of hope rose inside him like a tiny, fragile bubble. "Yes," he answered. "Holly's with Ludo up in his tree."

As Landon's party entered the ring, the Odds appeared to blink at them through the shadowy haze. *Do they notice anything different about tonight?* Landon wondered. Could they even see all the shadows gathering? They seemed intent on only one thing. The arrival of the Coin.

"We have to get to the tree," said Landon suddenly. He patted Ditty's arm as if she were dictating their direction. "To the tree. Your uncle's tree. Melech!"

"What about arrows?" asked Ditty, although she didn't sound too afraid.

"After what we've been through?" said Landon, showing a little more bravado than he was feeling. "They'll either miss or, if we become as hard as we did back there, they'll bounce right off."

Vates had leaned out to the other side as he began steering Melech around. "Is this phase two, Landon Snow?"

"It is," said Landon, "and we need to get my sister—fast."

"He-yaw!" Vates shouted, though Melech was already shifting into high gear. The Odds murmured disapprovingly, their voices soon stomped out by Melech's galloping hoofs. They sped toward the tree, cutting a line across the green.

Landon was amazed at Melech's speed and keen sense of direction. It was like he could smell that tree amid the darkness. Landon patted his sister's coat. *We're coming for you, Holly.*

As they approached the underside of the monstrous evergreen, Landon leaned toward Ditty. "How do we get inside? Is it still the same passwords?"

Ditty's hair bobbed. "Yes," she said, an amused edge to her voice. "I'll bet they are. Addlefoot's got no imagination whatsoever. And *nutmeg* and *ratchet* are his favorite words."

They neared the massive trunk, and Vates, who had apparently overheard Ditty's comment or knew about Addlefoot already, said in a commanding voice, "Nutmeg and ratchet! Nutmeg and ratchet!"

Landon thought he perceived some movement or sound above, but it was quickly followed by the loud rupturing of bark and wood. The tree was opening, though no light spilled out from within.

They trotted right in, and Landon covered his ears. Just when he was about to uncover them and see if the doorway was still open, he sensed it swinging shut and pressed his ears harder. *Whump!* The great tree and earth shook, rattling Landon's teeth and nearly springing him from Melech's back.

"I think I know what I'm supposed to do for the next part of the plan," Landon said, though he could hardly hear himself over the lingering din in his ears. Clutching Holly's coat to his side, he dismounted and stepped cautiously toward where he thought the staircase was that led up. He nearly tripped over a pile of heavy, rolled lengths of canvas or burlap. And he remembered the signs Ludo's nightly patrols brought in and stored here, the signs that spelled messages of warning, written by Vates and posted by Hardy. If he remembered correctly, Landon thought the pile seemed about the same height as during his last visit. Had Vates not posted any more messages since Landon's last visit? He could ask later. Right now there were more important matters at hand.

Vates and Ditty stepped to the floor behind him. Melech grunted and sniffed. "Dusty," he said.

A hand fell on Landon's shoulder, and he knew it was Vates's. Landon sighed. "I think I'm supposed to go get her alone." Vates's hand gently squeezed, and Landon sensed the old man was nodding.

"Sometimes a plan requires waiting. That will be Ditty's, Melech's, and my part now."

"Landon?" said Ditty.

He turned to face her, and though she was hard to see, he could tell she was standing near. "Ditty."

" 'Be strong and do not fear. Be of good cheer; the Auctor knows you are here.' "

Landon could tell she was quoting words that were not her own. Yet as she spoke them, they were her words, too. She believed what she was saying. They rang true, and they worked. Landon felt happy deep down. He wanted to hug her, but he merely smiled. "Yes," he said. "Thanks."

And with that, he stepped around the pile of banners and began to climb the stairs. He felt his way along the rough wood walls of the stairway, but though it was dark, he did not feel blind at all.

He had not been up these stairs before, though he assumed they must lead to Ludo's observation balcony.

Landon reached a landing and what seemed to be a hall or passage that led to the left. He crossed the hall and found another opening, a doorway that led to another set of stairs going up.

Before he reached the top, he instinctively slowed and listened. The air felt a touch cooler and was gently flowing, falling in his direction. The darkness, he realized, was moving. It was the creepiest thing to feel darkness, animated patches of black, moving around him and over him. Though it didn't seem possible, Landon gauged that it was late afternoon, a wintry dusk outside to those unaware of the shadows. The sky was dimming naturally to mesmerized eyes. Only Landon and his companions could see the cloaking of the shadows.

But not for long, Landon thought hopefully. What astonished him was how pervasive they were. The shadows were cloaking everything in darkness. Landon was tempted to quail. For one moment, he thought of turning back and running to hide in the darkness. But Ditty's words came back to him—"Be strong and do not fear"—and he climbed the final step, inching his way toward the opening on his right. The air grew chill, and Landon heard his sister's voice.

"What's wrong, Ludo? Look! Here it comes!"

Landon could detect the distant rumbling of the large wooden cart. The spoonlike catapult was being hauled onto the Echoing Green. He thought of Hardy and hoped he, too, was somehow fortified by Ditty's words, even from afar.

"Ah me, ah yes! Who am I to second guess? The great Coin is here, as always, and right on time. Then why do I feel a disturbance in my bones and in my—"

Rhyme? Landon wondered despite himself. *Mind?* He was

straining to hear, but the only sound was the faint rasp of his own breathing. He thought he detected the slightest of creaks in a board, just outside—

"You!" The word came in a shrill, small voice that ran down Landon like a long cold finger. "So you've returned to join the fun? Well, you must know you are no longer Second-to-None!"

An odd thing was happening. As Landon heard Ludo's voice and felt his nearness, the darkness began to drip away like black paint falling from a gray wall. Landon saw Ludo's face, his sharp nose only a nose away from his own. His eyes flickered and flashed so Landon could notice their striking blueness. Angular ears crested by orangish hair and a dark green top hat served to border the odd fellow's visage. Landon was feeling something strange yet somehow also familiar and inviting. For one thing, it was nice being able to see again!

"I'm not?" said Landon, his voice sounding somewhat distant to his own ears. "Then who?"

Ludo grinned, his teeth clamped tight as a jail cell. He turned his head, pointing with his nose and the tuft on his chin and his twiglike finger all at once. "Oh, you know who, don't you? Or does Ludo have to introduce you two?"

Landon and Holly stared at each other while Ludo giggled and took Landon's arm. "Come, come, don't be shy. Shake her hand, and just say hi."

Landon wanted to yank his arm away. He wanted to wriggle free of Ludo's talonlike grip. He wanted to. . .he wanted to. . .shake his sister's hand. "Hi," he heard himself say. Was he supposed to tell her his name, too? But she was his sister! Then again, she was Second-to-None, and that position did command some respect.

"Wait a minute!" Landon jerked his hand away from her. "Why should she be Second-to-None! That's what—that's who I was!" He turned on Ludo, wanting to shove him into the railing.

Ludo's smile grew broader. His voice dribbled with sweetness like syrup. He released Landon's arm and gently patted his shoulder. "There, there. Fair is fair. You had your chance and left your post. To find a suitable replacement, well, that's up to your host!" Ludo hooked his thumbs behind his lapels and flicked his fingers like bony piano keys.

"Ludo," said Holly, "I hate to interrupt. But isn't it time, you know, to read the Coin? I mean, the Odds are all gathered—one hundred and one percent of them, according to my calculation—and—"

Ludo spun on his heels and clamped his hands to his hips. "One hundred and *one*, Second-to-None? Such a percentage does not match our assemblage."

"Well," said Holly, bowing her head and sounding sheepish, "I rounded up. Precisely it's 100.5 percent. And I counted the other three, too. Sorry. I couldn't help it."

"The other three?" Ludo half turned to Landon, raising an eyebrow. "What other three? Come now, Second-to-None, you must speak clearly to me."

Holly peeked up and pointed at Landon. "Well, him, of course. And an old man with a white beard. And well, I counted the horse, too, so—"

Ludo raised his hand like a stop sign, and it had that effect. He slowly turned with his full gaze to Landon. When he was fully facing him, nose to nose and eye to eye, Ludo dropped his stop-sign hand and turned it palm up. "An old man," he said with a tic near his eye, "a horse—dark brown, I presume?" The tight skin at the corner of his mouth began to quiver. "And young Landon."

Ludo sighed deeply, almost affectionately, as he reached to take Landon by the shoulders. Ludo's fingers began to work into Landon's flesh until it felt like his bony fingertips were tapping Landon's shoulder blades. Landon felt his eyes tear up. Otherwise he couldn't move. After another deep sigh, Ludo twisted his mouth. "So, Second-to-None, my wonderful assistant and resident mathematician. You've given me cause to believe our attendance this evening is higher than the usual thousand Odds by five. A thousand and five, a percent of 100.5."

"Yes," said Holly, brightening. "That's correct."

"But you've given me only three identities. I request the other two, if you please." He let go one hand to snap his fingers, then returned them to Landon's shoulder, kneading.

"The other two are Odds, or were before you replaced their numbers in the Circle of Attendance. Their names were crossed off."

"And they are?" Ludo clapped his hands and grabbed Landon's shoulders.

"Ditty and Hardy."

For a moment, a rather long moment that seemed like several minutes, Ludo relaxed his hands and arms. His head drooped. Gravity seemed to be softening and pulling at his entire body. Landon was half expecting the poor fellow to drop to the deck like a sack of cloth. But gradually, slowly, he raised his head, top hat first, and held Landon with his steely blue gaze. Still, he said nothing.

Landon found himself breathing in shallow gasps. It felt like thick hands were pressing against his chest from front and back. Ludo released him completely and took a step back. Despite his dark glare, he looked defeated. Given up. *But given up to what?* Landon wondered. He had never felt so thoroughly confused in his life. Was he pulling for this poor hapless fellow? Rooting for him? Or was he against him? Hoping he would fail or fall or give up or whatever it was he was supposed to lose to. Why was Landon even up here? He blinked past Ludo and saw what appeared to be the very last light fading from a very hazy day. And what was Holly doing here? What were they all waiting for?

Holly peered at Landon. She looked to be in as much a fog as he was. She turned to Ludo and stepped toward him, closer to the rail. As she reached to touch the Odd, Landon wasn't sure, but he thought he noticed a dark, splotchy shape zip from the plank to her leg and up her back. *That was weird,* he thought. The thing, which was hardly any thing to speak of at all, was a disembodied shadow. *But no shadow has a body anyway,* he thought, smiling to himself. It was probably nothing. Landon shook his head.

There's another one.

This shadow squirmed as a snake, but faster. It had slithered from near where Landon was standing and zipped around Ludo's black, single-buckled shoe. And then, Landon was quite sure, the filmy shadow stretched up from the floor and disappeared in one of Ludo's coattails. *Okay,* Landon thought, *that was really weird. This is freaky.* He took a step back. Holly said in a soft yet urgent voice, "Ludo, they're all waiting. The circle is formed. The Coin is ready. Are you going to send it up now?" A worried look pursed her face as she glanced from Ludo to the green. The distant treetops were dimming like a dream.

"No," said Ludo.

Holly turned sharply, her hair swinging round like a whip. "What?"

Ludo had straightened, and he was leaning against the railing, his elbows propped behind him. He was looking at Landon.

"No," he said. "No reading of the Coin toni—er, I mean today, or at this time. No, no, no more reading of the Coin for Ludo!" He seemed to be perking up. "Find Wagglewhip or Trumplestump. Tell them to have the Coin removed from the green. Something has caused Ludo pain, and he has decided never to read from it again."

"But. . ." Holly sounded anguished, and Landon wanted to hold her or give her a hug. "Ludo. What will we do? What will we do?" It was the most pathetic cry Landon had ever heard. He could feel the ache in his heart, too. All of the Odds, his sister, him, not seeing the Coin rise and fall ever again. It was too much. What would they do?

"Go tell them," Ludo commanded. "Remove the Coin!"

Holly held up her hands in helplessness. "But—"

"Now, Holly! 1, 5, 29, 2, 64. . ." Ludo was glaring at her.

Holly gaped, seemingly immobile.

"1 plus 2 equals 7; 10 times 3 is 5; 4 minus 1 equals 11."

"Okay! Stop! I'll go," said Holly. She had put her hands over her ears and closed her eyes to shut out such mathematical atrocities. When she looked at him, Ludo arched an eyebrow and raised a finger. He opened his mouth. "I'm going," said Holly, her voice breaking. And without a glance at Landon, she stomped from the balcony.

Ludo watched her go, lowering his eyebrow and dropping his finger. Without turning his head, he narrowed his eyes and squinted at Landon. "You can't out-trick the trickster, Lan-duhn. Though I must say old Vates's presence is a surprise." He spat Vates's name. "The old coot and all his stinking lies. Right here on Ludo's territory, right here on my own turf. Yes, this is quite a turn of things; it shows a lot of nerve. Whatever plan you thought you'd schemed, I'm afraid it will not hatch. Because you see—and mind you, boy—for me you are no match!"

With instant clarity Landon remembered why he was here. He walked slowly and deliberately to the rail between Ludo and the megaphone. Looking out into the darkness over the vast circular clearing ringed by trees, Landon said, "I bet they're getting restless."

"Who's that? The Odds?" Ludo laughed. "Oh, they're never at rest. Which is how I like them best. And remember, Lan-duhn, how you also passed the test."

Ludo's elbow had slid off the railing, and he was fishing inside his coat. Landon tensed, waiting, feeling restless and anxious himself. He shifted Holly's jacket, which he still clutched to his side in his left hand. From the corner of his eye, he gauged Ludo's movement. Just when Ludo was bringing out his hand with something shiny in it, Landon half turned and swung as hard as he could.

His right hook connected with something hard and metallic, and he felt it break free from Ludo's grip. The object went sailing like a tiny comet, a gold fob trailing a gold chain. It was quickly swallowed by darkness, sinking like a pocket watch into the sea.

Landon took advantage of Ludo's momentarily stunned state by swinging Holly's jacket up and over his head, crashing it down on him with all his might. The top hat crumpled, and so did the bony little man beneath it, giving a tiny yelp. "Sorry," Landon blurted, quickly backing away. He was shaking. "It's the only way to help. I'm not attacking you."

Landon turned to the megaphone, grabbed the round, tapered end, and put his mouth to the hole. He aimed it downward but couldn't see anything below. He drew in a deep breath, almost choked on the cold, stale air coming through the cone, and shouted, "Heave!"

Nothing. Straining his ear, he knew what he secretly wanted to hear: *Ho, Landon Snow!* But no such reply came. At the very least, he thought the crowd would respond automatically, "Ho, Ludo!" How many years had they been offering such a chant? It was built-in, reflexive, almost second nature, wasn't it? He had seen all the Odds gathered around the green, waiting for that very word, *heave*. What was going on?

Landon tried again, his voice nearly cracking with the effort. "Heave!" No echo, not a sound. "Heave! Heave! Heave!" He was getting desperate, and Ludo was pulling Holly's jacket from his head. Licking his lips and shivering, Landon wondered what to do. This was the plan; he was sure of it. He had somehow fallen under Ludo's spell—or the shadows'—when he'd first heard Ludo's voice. And then Ludo's own words had led to his undoing, when he mentioned a "plan" that wouldn't hatch. *The plan!* Landon had thought. The plan that they were following, even though they weren't sure what it was until they got there. And now he was here, and Landon was sure this was where he was supposed to be.

At least he had been sure. Perhaps he was supposed to have gone with Holly? Ludo moaned and mumbled something, and much to Landon's increasing horror, the man giggled. He stood and popped out the top of his hat with his fist, seemingly unperturbed by Landon's actions, although his punches were extra swift and sharp.

"You think they'll listen to you?" He giggled again. "Oh, hee-hee-hee and hoo-hoo-hoo! I'm the reader, and they know my voice. I'm their leader, so they have no other choice." Ludo sighed. "Ah, yes, sounds like the Coin's been rolled away. Now step away from the cone, so they can hear what Ludo has to say."

Landon didn't move, except to lean his ear closer to the mouthpiece. He had turned his head to watch Ludo, and his ear had picked up something through the cone. It was faint, distant. But he thought he could hear voices. Ludo was brushing himself off and muttering something, and Landon wanted to shush him so he could better listen. Finally, he swiveled his head the other way, pressed his right ear to the hole, and heard a familiar voice crying, "No. Dat way! Back dere! Need to hoist and ho!" At least that's what Landon thought he heard. It sounded like Hardy.

Something was staring back at Landon from the corner of the balcony. Though there was no apparent light to see by, somehow one last ray from beyond the hidden horizon must have slipped through to strike this round, shiny eye just as Landon's gaze fell on it. It wasn't alive or animate. It wasn't a real eye at all. It was the shatterproof lens of Landon's flashlight.

It had winked and disappeared. Landon stared only a moment at the residual darkness before lunging blindly. He moved forward and down in one motion. And in that swift movement, a thought occurred to him: There is no such thing as a disembodied shadow. Every shadow comes from something. . .or someone.

Groping until his hand found the round, rigid casing, Landon lifted it, aimed, and fired. His first shot was at Ludo, who threw up his hands and stumbled back, a silent scream wrenching his face. Then Landon thrust the beam toward the green below. The column of light sifted the murky haze, at first finding nothing but darting, fleeing shadows. But as Landon stirred the air, scattering the darkness like grounds in coffee, some of the earth came into view far below. He searched and searched, sweeping the green back and forth, sweeping ever outward from the tree. When he heard a peep from Ludo's direction, he flashed the beam at him, startling him back against the wall.

Where are you, Hardy? Landon was sure he'd swept past the center of the green. Still there was no sign of Hardy or the catapult or other Odds. If this plan completely fell apart, the shadows would overcome everything and everyone. There would be never-ending darkness and chaos. It was unimaginable. Well, at least a couple days earlier it would have been. Now Landon knew what it was like to live in darkness, and he yearned more than anything to once again feel the sun warm his face.

A different sound, louder than the voices through the megaphone, rose to Landon's ear. He redirected the beam, and a low-flying shadow swooped from its glow. For some reason, Landon decided to chase it, and when he found it with the light, he was able to follow its path, keeping the light right on it as it moved. The noise rose up again. And Landon realized with awe that he was watching Melech racing and neighing across the green. Just when Landon thought Melech was sure to disappear into the woods, Melech slowed, and Landon passed the beam right over him. There it was. Melech had led him to the catapult and the great gold Coin.

It was too far away to see what was going on beneath the catapult. Trying to hold the flashlight steady, Landon waved his free hand around until it connected with a dangling lens. He pulled the lens to his eye and circled the light around until he found the Coin again. It glimmered from the beam, but it was so far away and the angle of light so low through the dark murky haze that the glimmer was nothing like its spectacular radiance when it was hoisted into a clear sky.

With the lens, Landon could see individuals. Hardy was in a skirmish with the other rope-pullers. They were clearly working to haul the Coin from the green. Hardy alone was fighting to turn it back. Holly had gotten word to Ludo's henchmen in record time. Landon noticed two figures charging at Hardy to rid him of his rope. Quite possibly these were Wagglewhip and Trumplestump themselves.

The tug of war seemed a lost cause. Persist as he might, Hardy was losing the battle, and in jerky fits and starts, perhaps advancing a foot or two at a time, the catapult was being dragged ever nearer the impenetrable cover of the woods.

The beam began to flicker. It blinked out, and Landon banged it on the rail. "Come on," he pleaded. "Not now!"

From the corner, Ludo giggled. Was it Ludo's voice or another that then whispered into Landon's ear, "You've given a valiant effort, and so have your friends. But in the end did you really think you could win?"

It wasn't Ludo's giggling Landon then heard, but a cacophonous chorus of laughter flitting and whirling and crawling and slinking all about him.

Chapter Fifteen

The flashlight's batteries were dying. Landon banged the flashlight against the railing three more times. With the third jolt, the light blinked and flickered to life. Closing one eye, Landon pressed the other to the dangling lens and aimed the glowing beam. Melech had entered the fray beneath the catapult, charging the Odds who clung to their ropes and were pulling the large contraption toward the woods. A few of them let go. One went swinging with his rope like a crazy pendulum. The remaining few were no match for Hardy. He wrested the catapult around and slowly brought it back onto the clearing. Melech had taken hold of a loose rope in his mouth and was adding his horsepower.

With this turn of events the shadows quit laughing around Landon. They seemed to have left the balcony. It was quiet. Passing through the shaft from his flashlight, Landon saw a thick dark mass crossing the green. The shadows were heading toward the catapult.

The flashlight dimmed, and then went out. Landon banged it but somehow knew it was no use. The batteries were dead.

"They're clear of the trees. It's safe now for the signal."

It was Vates. Landon felt relief at hearing his voice, but he didn't turn to look. He knew what he had to do. Letting go of the lens and setting down the flashlight, he moved to the megaphone in the pitch darkness and pressed his mouth to the narrow hole. "Heave, Hardy, heave!"

Since he could no longer see, Landon pressed his ear to the mouthpiece and listened. At first he heard only a faint, echoing whispery sound sort of like the sound of an ocean one hears in a large shell. But then he heard a grunt from Hardy and a snort from Melech. A sharp rumbling creak followed, and Landon imagined the lever was dropped and the spoon was up, thrusting the Coin into the blackest of nights. His heart ached to see it shine and flip with the dazzling radiance of a rainbow. But he knew it was best that he couldn't. Other voices were heard, shouts and grunts and pants. Landon tensed. The other Odds were coming back with the force of the converging shadows. Hardy's job was not yet done.

"Please," Landon heard Vates whisper, "strike true."

There was a scraping sound of steel against stone. *Shiiick. Shiiick.* And then a wonderful crackling pop. From the corner of his eye, Landon saw the distant spark fly. It was like someone had struck a match and tossed it into the air. But when this spark landed, it popped into three other sparks, like a small bouncing firework. The glowing orange dots turned yellow, and the yellow traveled like liquid in either direction, up and down the lever of the spoon until its complete upper side was illumined by soft fire.

Landon went to the lens and looked. Hardy was on Melech, and they were racing from the scene, soon disappearing from view in the darkness. They were headed back toward Ludo's tree. The fire continued to spread as the other Odds, the rope-pullers, gathered beneath it, staring up in shocked dread. "Get out of there," Landon whispered. Jumping back to the megaphone he hollered, "Run away! Go! Look out!"

The Odds scattered just in time. As the Coin came crashing down, the circle of Echoing Green lit up like the crater of an exploding volcano. Landon closed his eyes and turned away because it was so bright. When he looked back, the light had receded to the glowing mass of the giant Coin upon a crumpled heap of wood. The fire above the Coin shimmered in waves of blue and green and white like the Northern Lights. Then it flickered angrily with dancing, grappling flames of orange and yellow and red. It was the most amazing fire Landon had ever seen.

"Oh me, oh my! Why, why, why, why?"

In the wavering light, Landon saw Ludo sitting near the edge of the balcony, his legs thrust out beneath the bottom rail and his eyes peering between two higher slats. The flickering light made him glow in stripes, while his backside remained cloaked in shadow. The sharpness of his features drooped as if the fire were melting him rather than the Coin. He seemed oblivious to Landon and was soon blubbering like a small child. Landon couldn't bear to watch.

"So it happened, then," another voice said in an awed

tone. Ditty's form appeared and, for a split second, Landon thought he was gazing at her beneath a sparkling shower of fireworks. She smiled at him, but then she turned toward her uncle, and Landon could sense her heaviness. She took a step toward Ludo but stopped, Vates's hand upon her shoulder.

"Why don't you give him a minute. . .or two or three," Vates said soothingly. "Painful as this sight is for him, it is also setting him free. As the Coin melts, so will the hardness around his heart."

Landon turned around. "My sister!" he said, panic fluttering in his chest. "Has anyone seen. . ." He paused. Another figure emerged from the doorway. "Holly? Are you okay?"

She had on her hat and mittens and a light sweater, but her teeth were chattering. Her eyes were wide as headlights. Landon remembered her jacket and quickly crossed behind Ludo—who was crying more quietly now—to get it. He spread it open and draped it around his sister's shoulders, since her arms remained rigidly along her sides.

Landon rubbed her arms through the coat. "Holly? Can you hear me? It's Landon." The relief he'd felt at seeing her was being taken over by a new wave of rising panic. Holly took another couple of steps forward, and Ditty and Vates moved to either side as she advanced to the railing. She stood scarcely breathing, it seemed, for a good long while.

"It looks like a bonfire," she said at last. "Landon, are we camping? I don't remember this place. I feel like I've been having a really bad dream. Except. . .except. . ."

"Except what?" Landon asked gently.

"Except it didn't seem bad until now. I think it seemed

good, but it wasn't."

Landon swallowed a lump in his throat and hugged his sister, though she still remained rather rigid. "It was pretty bad, Holly. But I think it's starting to get better."

"It's not over yet," said Vates somberly. "The shadows seem to have scattered, at least for the moment. But this is only part one. Remember, Landon?"

Landon thought of the drawing depicting the three corresponding parts to his and Vates's visions. "The Coin is on fire," he said. But that had been the easiest part to figure out, since he had envisioned the Coin and Vates had foreseen a fire. It was strange, but since the pictures from his dream had actually been drawings done by Holly on a piece of wood, he wondered if perhaps somehow she had seen the same thing. "Do you remember a dream, Holly, where you were counting the fireflies in this tree—"

Landon felt her shiver between his hands. She began to slowly nod. "Except I don't think that was a dream. It seemed so real."

Eagerly, Landon went on. "And do you remember seeing me? Except I was a real, flying firefly?"

Holly began to shake her head. "No, Landon. You weren't there at all. I just counted them by myself."

"Oh." Landon sighed. So much for his sister helping to interpret his dream. He turned to Vates glumly. "The second part I saw was a dome between some trees. And you saw—"

"Tools," said Vates. "I only drew a few—I'm no artist." He smiled. "But what I really saw in my vision were lots and lots of tools. And I wonder if—"

"Tools," said Holly abruptly. "Lots and lots of tools.

Now where did I. . .Ah!" She turned around, shaking loose Landon's hands from her shoulders. "I did see lots of tools just yesterday, I think. But it seems like a long time ago." She made a funny frown.

"You saw tools?" Landon tried not to shout, he was so excited. "Where?"

Holly turned and said slyly, "I counted 455 tools, to be exact. And where were they? Hmm."

"It's important, Holly," said Landon, as if his urgency could compel her memory.

"In a storage shed," she whispered, but then she shook her head. "No, it wasn't a shed. It was a tree." Ludo cried and Holly jumped and glanced at him. "Uh-oh. I wasn't supposed to snoop. He's going to be mad."

"Don't worry about him," said Vates. "He's only going to be mad for a while. Now where was this tree?" Landon could tell Vates was curious, too.

"Not far," said Holly, still casting an unsure look Ludo's way. "It's right by the green."

"I see, I see." Vates nodded. "Landon? Do you see what I see?"

The first wave of smell came up from the clearing. Landon had never smelled burning gold before. It was kind of waxy smelling, like a big yellow candle. And there was a hint of burnt marshmallow.

In Vates's eyes Landon could see two fires. In those tiny reflections, though he couldn't actually distinguish the Coin from the flames, he imagined seeing it melting from a thick, giant disk into a thin, droopy shape. And then he thought of the tools.

"A dome," said Landon suddenly. "Part two of the plan is to build a dome from the gold of the Coin."

He'd forgotten he was staring into Vates's eyes, so when they crinkled and smiled, Landon flinched. "Very good," said Vates. "The time to strike will be soon, while the metal's still hot and malleable." The old man turned to Holly, who appeared to be only half listening. "Can you show me the tools?"

She blinked and nodded, still seemingly distracted by all the strange goings on around them.

To Landon, Vates said, "You will need to assemble the people and get them working as soon as we get the tools. With him down"—he glanced toward Ludo, who remained peering almost lifelessly out between the slats—"there will be a vacuum in leadership," Vates took hold of Landon's shoulders and leaned closer. "They must build that dome."

Landon blinked. He struggled to return Vates's gaze, so intense were the old man's eyes. Landon's heart fluttered, and his knees weakened. Finally, in what felt and sounded more like a croak than a reply, he said, "Okay."

"Good." Vates gently squeezed his shoulders and then let go. "Holly, please show me that tree. And Landon, remember Ditty's words."

Landon frowned and glanced at Ditty. She merely smiled with her mouth closed, and Landon's frown faded. *Be strong and do not fear. Be of good cheer; the Auctor knows you are here.*

"This is Ditty?" said Holly abruptly. Turning, she said, "Hi, I'm Holly. Landon's sister. Pleased to meet you!" Ditty returned the greeting, and the two girls shook hands. Holly spun around with a wry smile on her face. "She is cute,

Landon," she said softly but not softly enough. "I approve." Before stepping inside the branch corridor behind Vates, Holly paused and turned back. "You should give her a Valentine." She grinned and was gone.

Landon could feel Ditty watching him. "A Valentine? What is that?"

Landon swallowed. He pretended the rush of warmth in his face was from the blaze across the green, although he knew they were too far from it to feel the heat.

"Um," he said. Suddenly he was back in Ms. Gillersby's room surrounded by pink and red and white hearts. And there was the big heart up front with the calendar on it. "It's um, like a heart."

She didn't step closer, but it sure felt like she did. Was she leaning toward him? Landon wished Ditty would look away. His heart was beating furiously.

"Hm," she said finally. And then in a soft mutter, as if talking to herself, "Like a heart."

Landon's brain was turning cartwheels. He was supposed to do something, something important. But whatever it was, it was buried beneath a pile of red and white and pink hearts. Ditty, mercifully, took a step back. Landon glanced up shyly, happy to be able to breathe again. Ditty had never looked so cute, simply standing there in the blinking light. She raised her hands and clapped, twice. "Call them," she said. "Gather the people."

"That's right," said Landon, "we have to make a dome!" He jumped to the megaphone and directed it downward. "People of the valley! Woodfolk round the Echoing Green!" He paused for an echo that wasn't there, and prayed the people could hear him. "You are no longer Odds! I repeat—"

"Augh!" An anguished cry pierced the air. Ludo's hands were still stuck through the railing slats, but his head hung between his arms. It was bobbing, so his next cry rose and fell in waves. "Aw–wah–aw–wah–awds!" He continued muttering and crying incoherently, and Landon pressed on, raising his voice.

"You aren't Odds! You're people! Woodfolk! Craftsmen and—and. . ." What else had Ditty said about them? Landon couldn't think of the words. Besides, tonight they would need metal smiths above the other trades. "And craftswomen, too! We need you to remember your skills, collect your tools, and make a golden dome over Echoing Green. Report to the tool tree! And then follow me!"

Landon stepped back from the megaphone. He felt dizzy and weak and light-headed and exhausted. Had they heard him? Would they do what he said? And would they remember how to use their tools? What if they hadn't changed at all? As spellbound Odds, they would be no good. They had to remember. They had to be able to think for themselves. Landon certainly didn't know how to sculpt metal. He had never had a metalworking class. But just as his doubts were about to overwhelm him, a cry rose up from below.

"To de tool tree!"

An anxious moment passed before the boisterous echo.

"To the tool tree!"

"He won't fool me!"

"He won't fool me!"

"Remender your skill!"

"Remember your skill!"

"To do de Auctor's will!"

"To do the Auctor's will!"

Landon's heart leaped at the sound. When Ditty took his hand and led him through the branch and down the tree, neither the darkest shadows nor the loudest wails from Ludo could quench his joy.

At the tool tree, the men—and some women and older boys—were clambering for their old implements like fish fighting for food. Holly was standing on a stool, handing out the various hammers and chisels and saws, while Vates stood to one side directing traffic. "Pounders here. Shapers over here. Cutters right there. And drillers back behind the tree." He glanced up, spotting Ditty and Landon at the back of the crowd. "You'll need carpenters, too!"

Landon was tempted to look behind him, but he knew Vates was speaking to him. Some of his next words were lost to the hubbub, but Landon caught enough to figure it out. "Catapult. . .rebuild. . .scaffold. . .reach high. . .dome!" Then Vates continued organizing the groups.

"We need to build a scaffold," Landon said to Ditty, "so they can get up to the high parts inside the dome. Where's Hardy and Melech?"

Ditty tapped Landon's shoulder, and he looked. The duo raced in from the green and, with Hardy turned sideways and reaching down both hands, scooped up Ditty and Landon. Landon thought his arm had been yanked right from its socket. The next thing he knew, he was seated in front of Hardy while Ditty had been plopped behind the two of them. And so they were off across the green, galloping through a haze of smoke and darkness. If shadows were looming about,

Landon could neither see them nor sense them. His mind was preoccupied enough with the mission before him.

The fire was nearly out, and the once great Coin lay spread before them like a dripping, steaming mass of molten lava. It still glowed a golden hue but not nearly so brightly or brilliantly as it had in the blaze. The large rugged cart, Landon noticed in amazement, was still intact. The wooden wheels, the flatbed, and even the two vertical supports were mostly there. The spoon itself had largely crumbled. A new structure would have to be built to raise workers—as well as sheets of gold, most likely, Landon realized—to complete the ceiling of the dome.

Deep down, Landon understood the craziness—not to mention the sheer immensity—of the situation. The fact that he was somehow in charge of this project was the most ridiculous part of all. Yet he was riding on something much bigger than himself (and not just Melech). Something much, much larger than the idea of building a dome of gold in the middle of the night was carrying him along. Landon knew he wasn't really in charge. As crazy and ridiculous and big as the mission was, Landon believed it could happen. Because somehow, in some mysterious and seemingly miraculous way, the Auctor was involved. *He knows I'm here,* Landon thought, *because He's here, too.*

Landon felt a tap on his shoulder so light, he almost failed to notice it. Turning his head, he saw a little bird perched there.

"Hi, Epops," Landon said.

"Twee-too!" Epops tilted his head, and his black eyes shone.

A faint tremor became a dull rumble. Landon craned his neck and looked back. Through the patches and foggy rags of what appeared a forsaken battlefield, a mass of figures emerged. They were soldiers—fairly short soldiers—armed with crude instruments. They were coming not to destroy but to build for a battle that was yet to come.

We're going to fight the shadows, Landon thought. *The shadows of Malus Quidam.*

Chapter Sixteen

I n what seemed like a mystical dream, Landon sat upon
Melech and rode to and fro like a general. He issued
commands, motivated the troops, and on the whole oversaw
the construction of a makeshift scaffold, a massive dome, and
a hoist to raise and lower the dome from one side.

Nearly everyone else was working. Those without tools
were busy moving pieces around, holding things up, and
shuttling jugs of water back and forth from some unseen
well. Landon's commands, however, were mostly instructions
being passed on from Vates or Hardy or Wagglewhip and
a few other former Odds who really knew what they were
doing. Also, Landon motivated the troops by reacting to what
they had already done. When he saw the first two gold sheets
raised and fitted and hammered and welded, Landon clapped
with glee. "Good job!" he shouted. "Great!"

One crew carried blowtorches similar to Vates's lantern
with the directional disk. The difference was that these

"lanterns" had pointed steel funnels on top, which shot out a tiny blue flame.

"Amazing!" said Landon, his voice getting hoarse. He didn't care about his throat. The dome was going up!

Of course, not everyone was directly involved. A number of womenfolk stood watching and restraining their children along the tree line. Landon didn't see Ditty or Holly among them. Feeling a twinge of concern, he was about to call out for them, but his voice merely cracked toward oblivion. "Holl. . .Dit. . ." It was no use. Where were they?

He should have known. He spotted Holly briskly walking between sheet cutters and welders. She had out her notepad, pen, and calculator. Even as she walked, her head was bent over, and she appeared to be making notations. Was she counting the sections of gold sheeting? Or was she calculating the piece sizes and curvature and diameter of the dome? Probably, Landon thought, she was doing all those things. He couldn't help feeling proud of her mathematical brilliance.

And Ditty? There she was—off by herself, although close enough to both the construction zone and the trees to be easily included with either crowd. Her leather pack rested against her knee, and on her lap, a book lay open. Landon closed his eyes a moment, as if he could hear her murmurings. He couldn't hear her words, of course, but in one split second of silence among the battering and banging and cutting and fusing, he did hear something else.

"Twee-too!"

Epops's call came from high overhead. A two-tone song that somehow seemed to capture the essence of all that was happening—the construction, the preparation, the watching, the waiting—and distill it into those two notes. Landon heard Epops's call, and then it was gone, drowned out by the surrounding noise. As long as the green bird circled overhead, Landon felt assured that they were safe.

The dome was put up in record time (not that there had been a previous record that anyone was aware of). Perhaps all that time of doing nothing but watching a gold Coin flipping twice a day had the valley people pent up to get back to work and do something constructive.

Landon watched from his mount on Melech as the last worker rappelled down the slope of the dome from the top. Freshly twisted ropes ran through a system of pulleys, from the bottom edge of the dome to the north (toward the river and Vates's place), up to the top, and then to the east into the giant pine (formerly "Ludo's tree"). The ropes ran between the vertical posts of the balcony through the branch corridor and down the stairway, all the way to the base of the trunk. All along the route inside the tree were men, many of them former rope-pullers of the spoon catapult. Exhausted as they were from the intense construction (and even the former rope-pullers weren't used to working more than six pulls a day), they needed a lot more manpower to raise the dome.

From outside the dome, the brushing and scraping that were going on inside only sounded like muffled rubbing. Inside, however, Landon knew the noise must be deafening. Using the scaffolding for elevation and pads that looked like steel wool, workers were burnishing the dome's interior, smoothing every soldered seam and welded ridge until it seemed the dome had been formed from a mold. When the scratching finally stopped, the faintest hum reverberated from the round gold shell. Now they were rubbing the inside with cloth and oil. It was vital that the interior have a luster purer than a mirror.

As the last ring of sound faded to silence, Landon felt a weight of expectation press against his chest. He took a deep breath, cleared his throat, and spoke in as loud and clear a voice as he could muster. "Hoist the dome!"

From inside the pine and from high overhead, a chorus rang out. "Ho! Ropes! Pull!"

The ropes groaned like a rolling wooden ship, and the lip of the dome began to rise, as a lid about to reveal a giant gourmet meal. Inside was not a steaming filet mignon or a sizzling flambé, however, but about a hundred workers, a scaffold, and Landon's sister.

Holly emerged first with her mittens rolled and held against her ears by the tied-down flaps of her hat. She had entered the dome this way to protect her ears from the din of the scraping and scratching. She had probably just forgotten to take them off. Landon smiled at her as she approached. Again he felt that surge of pride. *She was part of the plan all along. She was left here—instead of going to Vates's with me—so that she could find out where the tools were stored. And maybe. . .maybe she was here for some other reason, too.*

Landon didn't know what that other reason might be. It used to bother him when he didn't understand something or couldn't figure out a reason for it. But he was beginning to trust in something beyond his understanding. This whole "plan," he realized, wasn't his plan or even Vates's. It was the Auctor's. And when Vates said Landon was to be the one to come up with it, it wasn't that he was supposed to actually come up with a plan so much as come to trust in the One who had the plan. Landon had a feeling the Auctor had had a plan all along. The only way to learn the plan, Landon discovered, was simply to step out—to act—believing the plan was there.

"Well, that was something!" Holly shouted from two feet away.

Landon flinched and grinned, covering his ears and squeezing them to indicate Holly's earmuffs.

"Oh!" she shouted again, and then she undid the string beneath her chin and removed her hat. Her mittens fell out, and she picked them up.

"So how's it look in there?" asked Landon.

The scaffold had been dismantled and was being removed in parts. The dome had continued to rise until it rested at a forty-five-degree angle. Holly looked at it, tilted her head forty-five degrees, and turned back with an approving look on her face. "Looks good," she said.

Landon climbed down from Melech. He was holding his flashlight, which hadn't burned since the batteries had died hours ago.

"Now what?" asked Holly. Vates, Ditty, and some other folk were gathering round. Landon scanned the unfamiliar faces and paused to look at Vates and Ditty. They both gave him slight smiles but looked serious, too. Landon sensed something of import was about to happen. And whatever it was, he was to be part of the plan.

"Now comes the hard part," said Landon. "It looks like the shadows have left us alone. . .for now." He realized this probably sounded kind of silly, as it was dark out and shadows could easily hide. Yet nobody smiled or laughed. It seemed they all knew or could sense something.

Landon sighed. Hardy was up in the tree, helping direct the rope-hoisting operation. Landon would have liked Hardy's stolid character with him for what he had to do next.

Vates, well, Vates had done his part—getting Landon here.

Ditty—she had her book, and she would pray, Landon knew, to give him strength.

Melech swung his head toward Landon and nuzzled his shoulder. Landon glanced at the ground, remembering all the times in his previous adventure when Melech had saved him. Landon so much wanted to climb back aboard this great horse and take him into the woods with him. But he knew what he had to do.

"I'll go, too."

A soft touch on his other arm came from a mittened hand. Landon looked up. Holly had put her hat and mittens back on in their proper fashion, although the earflap strings hung loosely to either side. Landon's stomach tightened. He wanted to say no, but something restrained his voice. He looked hard at his sister.

"We came down here together—almost." Holly smiled meekly. "I'm not even sure what we're doing—this is all so crazy. But I think I should come with you."

Landon looked at his sister and smiled back. "Yes. Yes, we'll go together." He nodded and held up his flashlight. "I just wish this thing still worked. It's dark out there." He glanced warily toward the silent forest. Somewhere out there waited a legion of shadows.

"Here." Holly took the flashlight, unscrewed the end, dropped out the two large batteries, reversed them, and put it back together. She clicked it, and a dim light shone forth. She immediately turned it out. "Squeezes out a little more juice," she said.

"Holly," said Landon, "you're a genius."

She snorted and rolled her eyes, handing him the flashlight. Melech snorted, too, in what sounded like a mimic of Holly's, and then he apologized. "Excuse me. You have a brave sister, Landon."

Landon sighed. A faint glimmer glistened from Melech's eyes. "I am about to do my duty, Melech." Landon patted the horse's head. "And I hope I'll be glad for it."

"This is still part two of the plan," said Vates, stepping forward. "Remember?"

Landon thought. Part one was the Coin burning. Part two was the dome, which was now up and lifted like a trap. And part three? Those strange shapes that looked somehow like pieces of a puzzle.

"I guess we won't know part three until this part is done," said Landon. He looked at Vates, seeing the raised dome behind him. Ditty broke into the little group and hugged Landon. "This may help your eyes for a time," she said, tapping the flashlight. "But these words will help your heart always." She took a half step back and opened the book.

There is no way she can read it, Landon thought. The lanterns had all been dimmed or gone completely out around them. He was about to turn on the flashlight when she began to speak.

" 'His light will show you the way. His brightness will reveal your path. And his glory will be reflected as you follow his plan.' "

Landon knew Ditty was speaking from memory, quoting the *Book of Illumination* by heart. She had finished by looking at him, not at the book. Ditty closed the book and gave him another hug. Then she hugged Holly and stepped back. Everything around Landon was growing darker. The dome was fading. Faces were becoming indistinguishable. What little light there had been was being pressed out like moisture from a sponge. Landon shuddered.

Clamping the flashlight under his armpit, Landon fished his gloves out of a jacket pocket and put them on. He took Holly gently by the elbow as the gathering of bodies parted to make way. "Come on," Landon whispered, feeling the hoarseness rasping his throat. "Let's go."

Landon and Holly stayed close together as they made their way into the black woods. They bumped into trees and bushes, each time experiencing momentary panic that they'd become separated. And each time Landon was tempted to turn on his flashlight, only to find his sister again as he called her name and listened for her response. "Here," she'd say softly. "I'm right here." And there she was just inches away. But in this profound darkness, an inch could have been a mile.

"What is it we're looking for?" Holly asked.

"Oomph," said Landon, knocking against a trunk of rough bark. "Holly?"

"Here I am."

"Shadows," said Landon. "More than looking for them, we're hoping to be. . .to be—" he swallowed.

"Yes?"

"To be found by them. And followed. Holly, we're the bait. I think."

"Oh."

The forest floor quietly crunched beneath their feet. Landon stopped, feeling Holly bump his arm. Nothing had changed around them visibly; it was so dark the only change could have come from light. But Landon had sensed something. Something cold and hollow. It felt as if the air were gently sucking or pulling at them. Landon's shudder turned to a prickly, tingling sensation that plucked all over his skin. His body was telling him to turn back and run. *Use the flashlight, turn around, and run!* His mind was in agreement, for that matter. So what held him here? *The plan,* he thought in some place deeper than his mind. *This is part two, and I've got to see it through.*

Holly tapped his elbow as lightly as a brushing leaf. Landon felt for her arm and then found her mittened hand. He guided her forward with him, step by awful step, not sure what they were heading into or toward, other than that it felt like a huge nest of swarming shadows.

"That's it, that's it. Come with me, and you'll be able to truly see! Did Vates say there was a plan? A plan?" The voice gently laughed. "And you believed him? Or what exactly did you believe? What do you believe now, Landon Snow? Yesss. . .yesss. I know your name. And so much more. Follow me, and I'll show you a real plan. A plan that puts you on top. A plan that everyone will love. A plan for power and riches and happiness and—"

Something squeezed Landon's hand, and he jerked it away. He was beginning to feel strangely warm. His mind was buzzing with this voice. It wasn't just what it was saying to him, though that was starting to sound pretty good to him, too. It was something more, something about the voice itself that grew on him. The longer he listened, the more he felt inclined to follow—

"Landon! Where'd you go? What are you doing?"

Landon stopped, lost. He felt dizzy now, truly, faintingly dizzy. Where was he? What was he doing? Those were two good questions to consider.

"Don't stop now. Just a few more steps, and I'll show you the way to your true purpose. Come with me, and you will be free of this darkness forever."

"Holly," said Landon, though it hardly seemed like his own voice speaking. "I just want to see something. Just a couple more steps. I'll be right back. Wait here."

"See something? Landon, how can you see anything? It's completely dark. In fact—"

Her voice broke off. Just when Landon was about to take another step into the invisible denseness of shadows, Holly's voice came back like a distant echo.

"I'm scared."

Landon stopped. It felt like he had one foot up in midair, though he couldn't see it. What was he doing? Two strange waves of fear clashed within him, flooding his soul. He was afraid not to give in to the voice from the shadows. It would be so easy, so nice to just follow it and do what it said. But another, contrary fear was beginning to push him back. What if he did give in and not finish the plan? Would he ever return? What would happen to him? And what would happen to the others? To the valley people, to Vates, Hardy, Melech, and Ditty.

"I'm so confused!" Landon wanted to shout, though he felt

something tight constricting his throat like a soft, furry hand. "Holly!" he croaked. "What are you doing? Let go of me!"

"Landon!" It sounded like Holly was crying, and her voice didn't seem close enough for her to be touching him, let alone strangling him. "I'm really scared! Please. . ."

And then Landon saw it. It's hard to describe precisely what it was, but what Landon saw vaguely resembled a tree— a tree made only of darkness. And the tree was looking at him with two eyes like slits. Its whole body was waving gently to and fro. As Landon drew near, however, he could sense the tornado seething within. It was a swirling mass of shadows, a visage of Malus Quidam.

Landon felt something flicker inside him. *Ditty is praying for me,* he thought. *She's asking the Auctor for help.* And then Landon, too, closed his eyes and turned his face upward. In the next instant he was turned around.

"Holly," he said clearly, marveling at the return of his voice.

"I'm here." She stood at his side, touching his arm.

A thrilling sense of calm welled up inside Landon. He flipped on the flashlight and winced at the glare. Trees with frozen leaves loomed from the darkness, their shadows stretching back innocently from the light. A leaf appeared to fall, but then it fluttered onward. It wasn't a leaf but a shadow from behind them, a piece of Malus Quidam flying on ahead.

"We've got to hurry," said Landon. "We need to beat him back, whatever he is."

An eerie voice quietly laughed. The shadow-bat had circled and was flapping about their heads. Soon there would be a swarm of them. Landon sensed fast-moving shadow-snakes zipping near their feet. He tried not to think of the black wolf figures he was sure were loping alongside from tree to tree. "Come on!"

With the bouncing spray of light leading the way, Landon and Holly were able to run full out, splitting to dodge trees and then coming back elbow-to-elbow. Landon knew it was important not to look back. Part of him kept niggling that he really should take just one more peek. *No!* he told himself, forcing his eyes to keep straight ahead. Amid his panting breaths and lunging feet and pumping arms, some words came to him. *Keep your eyes on the path set before you. Run the race marked out for you. Do not let the darkness drag you back. Do not give in to the shadows, and so stumble and fall.*

The flashlight blinked, and Landon skidded, afraid he was about to ram a tree. The light came back on, and Landon could see the trees yielding before them. Beyond the trees yawned a cavernous space. Landon brought the flashlight up, and its beam caught the high, receding arc of the inside of the dome in a burst of golden light—and then the light flickered out.

The swift change from light to dark left Landon blinded. He was still running forward onto the grass of Echoing Green, into the space beneath the poised dome. He slowed to a jog in the darkness, groping at the air. "Holly?" His voice faintly rang and echoed back from above.

"I'm here," she said softly, her own voice rippling like spreading circles on water.

Landon stopped. He slapped the flashlight twice but knew the batteries were dead. He let the flashlight fall to the ground. He rested on his knees, panting. "Holly," he said between breaths. He was breathing hard from the run but also from a sudden growing anticipation of what was to come. "This is it."

"Are you scared, Landon?" Holly's voice quavered.

"Yes."

They waited in a silence that seemed to echo itself, as the space beneath the dome became blacker and blacker. Well, the plan seemed to have worked to this point. Landon and Holly had succeeded in gathering the shadows beneath the dome. In the midst of the dense darkness, where Landon thought he might choke it was so thick, he and his sister could only wait. For what, he wasn't sure. When Landon heard a loud groaning and sensed that the dome was beginning to drop, he wondered if he and Holly might become trapped with Malus Quidam. . .forever.

Chapter Seventeen

It couldn't be said that they glowed, for they emitted no light. But somehow in that mass of overlapping shadows, Landon saw two slitlike eyes approaching, boring down on him. There were no other discernible features, yet somehow the eyes seemed to be smiling. *It* was smiling. *He* was smiling. Malus Quidam had Landon and Holly trapped inside an impenetrable sheath. Even if the sun were to shine—or even the moon or stars—no radiance could pierce the gold shell, nor sneak beneath its laden rim.

The plan didn't make sense. Had it ever, really? Landon suddenly thought he had been duped all along. Vates had been in on it, hadn't he? He and Ludo had probably planned this together from the start. That would mean Hardy, Melech, and Ditty, too, would have known about this trap. Landon couldn't believe how betrayed he had been. *Why did I ever trust them?* he thought, a pain stabbing his heart like a knife. *If I ever get out of here, I'll show them! They'll be sorry we ever met!*

But were these really Landon's thoughts? He couldn't see; nor could he think straight. All he could hear was a dull, throbbing, hissing ring. He thought he would go mad in this place. Except this wasn't a place, was it? It was nothingness. Emptiness. Loneliness, despair, oblivion.

Landon fell to the ground. He flailed his arms and legs, beating against the invisible earth. And then he stopped, panting but no longer caring. It didn't matter. Darkness had come. It had overwhelmed him. It had won. There was no one—or nothing—else. *I don't care,* he thought, wondering if he was speaking into the dirt or only thinking.

Landon was about to die. There seemed no other possibility. It was inevitable. It seemed, in fact, that he was being swallowed by death. It was not only all about him; it had somehow gotten inside him. Like a nasty worm inside an apple, the darkness was rooting around in him, eating away at the core of his being. *It's only a matter of time,* Landon thought. And just when he was about to give up all hope, something happened.

A sound, both strange and familiar, caught his ear. It was the two-note song of a bird. *Epops!*

Another sound followed, a voice also strange and familiar. An image came to Landon's mind of a sprightly sprig of a fellow dressed in dark green and wearing a top hat. Ludo? What could he be doing here?

Ludo was screaming. His shrill cry filled the void. Apparently the dome had not yet completely closed, and through the diminishing gap had entered both the green bird Epops and the green-clad figure of Ludo. Landon raised his head, seeing nothing but sensing movement. What was going on?

"Aaauuugghh! They're after me! I swing and I slug, but I can't escape the bug!" Ludo's voice bounced around the dark arena.

In one of the strangest sights Landon had ever seen, the floating, slitlike eyes flared first in surprise and then in what seemed horror. The tall, narrow pupils had shifted from Landon to focus somewhere else. Around the eyes and below them, Landon saw first a crooked, twisted tree. Its branches seemed to curl and drip and glide away like snakes. Then it sprouted leaves, which flew off in waves like so many bats plunging toward the sky. And then from its trunk leaped creatures each with a head and a tail and four legs. The wolf-shadows ran about in circles, and jumped back and forth as if confused about where to go. In a word, Landon realized, they looked trapped.

"No!" a hissing, growling voice bellowed. But it was gone without an echo, and Landon wondered if only he had heard it. Still lying prostrate, Landon turned his head to follow the weird eyes' gaze. He found nothing but crazily shifting shadows. Yet his ears detected something else. The tiny hum of an insect.

The whining seemed small like a mosquito. But Landon sensed it was still far away. Within moments, the whine had become a drone that soon grew to a steady buzz. Whatever it was, there was now more than one of them. The air became charged. The crackling *whirr* was everywhere; the dome hummed with reverberations. And through this tremulous din came the call of Epops—not loud or raucous but painfully sweet and clear.

"Twee-too! Twee-too!"

The earth shook with the closing of the dome.

And then someone turned on the lights.

From pitch darkness to pure brightness, Landon was sure he would never be able to see again. He shielded his eyes, but it was no use. Even totally covering them with his hands didn't keep out the light. There was no escaping it. A golden glow flooded everywhere. And Landon knew: The plan was brilliant.

Eventually, miraculously it seemed, his eyes adjusted. Forms came into view accompanying the sounds. The forms were dots of light—buzzing and flitting and zipping in every direction. Landon rolled onto his back and gazed in wonder at what could have been a thousand living, shooting stars against a sky of shimmering amber. There was not a hint of darkness anywhere, not even a shadow. Where could one possibly exist inside this dome of golden light? There was no spot to dim, no corner to darken, no object to hide behind. Epops was circling. Ludo had gone down somewhere, lying facedown or up, Landon wasn't sure. And Holly?

Landon was about to turn, concerned for his sister, when he felt something brush his hand. "I'm here," came her voice. And there she was, smiling. Landon wanted to laugh. His hands felt warm, and he realized he was still wearing his gloves. He pulled them off and set them aside. Then he found Holly's hand—her mittens were off, as well—and held it, watching the dazzling flight of the fireflies.

Landon could have lain there forever, gazing at the fireflies. It was like watching a hundred fireworks at once, fireworks that did not dip and fade away but continued to rise and circle and buzz and soar. "It's like a fountain of gold," he heard Holly quietly say, giving his hand a gentle squeeze. *This is true, too,* Landon thought. The fireflies were drops of light bouncing and splashing against an upturned bowl of gold.

"It's like," Landon said, and then he paused, wondering if he was about to fall asleep beneath this twinkling honey sky. His body indeed felt heavy. It felt so good to just lie here, soaking up the light. His muscles relaxed for the first time in what had seemed days. He felt exhausted, but it was a good exhaustion. A sweet, wonderful, sleepy. . .

Landon's eyelids drooped. When he opened them, he noticed something else was opening, as well. A groan sounded from high overhead like that of a big iron ship. Then a fresh breeze brushed over Landon. The coolness of it was invigorating. Landon turned his head. The bottom edge of the dome was lifting. He tried to sit up, but he was too tired. The dome kept rising, tilting backward from the ground.

Landon momentarily stiffened, wondering if a shadow from outside might slip in and invade this wonderful light, might again darken the sky like a cloak. But no darkness slipped in. In fact—and Landon was staring wide-eyed despite his weariness—the air outside was not dark. The golden glow from within the dome seemed to spill out and infuse the world with brightness.

Soon there was no difference between the light within the dome and that without. Everything was light. Then the dome rose above the treetops, and Landon squeezed his sister's hand and felt her doing the same to his. They were both gasping at a sight they had not seen since entering this hazy world: the blue sky. And there was the sun.

"It's morning," Landon finally said in amazement,

blinking. "After a long, long night."

The fireflies took to the air—a thousand tiny stars strangely visible against the wide light of day. "It's like," Landon said again, fighting the weariness but then giving in. "It's like. . .a miracle." And then he closed his eyes, and he slept.

Chapter Eighteen

When Landon awoke, he thought he must be dreaming. Above him floated oddly curved shapes, all in gold. They hung at different levels, and each one was distinct from the rest. Yet somehow they all seemed to fit together. Gradually Landon's ears began to work, and sounds—voices mostly—began to draw near. A draft of air stirred past him, and the large gold shapes began to gently swirl. It was a beautiful, colossal mobile, like something one might find hanging over the foyer in an art museum.

"Hi, Landon."

Landon turned. A stiffness in his neck told him he'd probably been lying still on his back for several hours. He quickly forgot about the stiffness, however, when his eyes focused on the face that was looking at him. She was smiling.

"Ditty." That one word was enough. Landon felt himself smiling back. "Ditty."

She looked up. "Aren't they beautiful? The valley people

were still so wound up and excited that they worked all day dismantling the dome and turning it, well, into this." She raised her hand, and then brought it down and looked at Landon. "Vates told me about your visions and his dreams. That you and he did see the plan, even if you didn't understand it until it unfolded before us."

Landon looked at the shapes and breathed. He thought of the sketches he'd seen in his dream, sketches he'd thought Holly had scribbled at the time. He laughed to himself. "The Coin," he said, glancing at Ditty.

"Had to burn," she said.

"And the dome. . ."

"Had to be built."

"And. . ." Landon paused, placing his hands behind his head and flexing his shoulders. "And these shapes. . ." He watched them twist and twirl, admiring their artistry and design.

"Had to be here when you woke up to see them."

Ditty was beaming, and when Landon looked at her again, he felt a jab in his heart. It felt good. He wanted to say, "You're the cutest girl I know." He yearned to say, "I really, really like you, Ditty." The longer he looked at her, however, the tighter his throat clamped up. Finally, it was all he could do just to swallow. And then, with warmth flooding his face and his heart pounding so hard it might burst, Landon managed to say, rather squeakily, "Ditty?"

Her eyes shone as she leaned closer, her hair dangling precariously near his face. "Landon?"

"Thanks," he said, glancing slightly away.

Ditty sighed, and she tapped him twice softly on the nose.

"You, too," she said.

"Ah, Landon." It was Vates. He approached preceded by one thump and then another thump of wood upon wood. Landon looked up, his back aching. He lay back down with a groan.

"You need a hand?" Vates was standing over him, one gnarled hand grasping a walking staff, the other reaching out to Landon. As Landon took it, he heard clapping behind him. A dull, thick-sounding clap: *thup, thup, thup!*

There was Hardy, grinning and drooling and slapping his mitts together. "We did it!" he said, holding his hands together a moment to wink that sly, knowing wink of his. And then he resumed clapping.

Landon laughed. "We did it," he said, eyeing the three of them with affection. He nodded slowly, easing his stiff neck back into motion. "We did it."

Now that he was sitting up, Landon looked about him. This place seemed oddly familiar yet completely new and different. The ceiling was composed of arched tree roots—or inwardly growing branches—crossing back and forth like crooked rafters.

Landon was sitting on a hard wood table, though there was a rolled out canvas beneath him. Dozens more tables and chairs were scattered about. Many of them were filled with valley folk, who were talking and drinking from mugs and laughing and smiling. Beyond them, at the far end of the room, was a bar with gleaming glass cabinets behind it. A bartender was sliding mugs across the bar.

"Ginger ale up!" came the shout. A hand from seemingly nowhere grasped the mug at the last instant and hoisted it in among the throng.

Landon shook his head. His eyes passed over Hardy, Vates, and Ditty, who were smiling at him. But Landon hardly noticed them. His attention was taken by a column of rough wood standing nearby. It was a support running all the way up to the ceiling, and from it, four beams spread horizontally to other posts in the room. But it was what was on the column that had caught Landon's eye. Or what was hanging from it, rather, upon a rusted nail: an empty lantern.

Landon looked at Ditty. She seemed to be enjoying this very much. She glanced at the lantern and then turned and smiled at Landon. Her eyes glistened, and her smile softened to something deeper, an expression more profound. And she nodded.

"That's the lantern," Landon said slowly, his mind trying to reconcile this time and place with the one he was remembering from only months ago, "that you plucked the firefly from. It was in a bubble. Sleeping. And you. . .you gave it to me." Landon held an imaginary bubble between his thumb and forefinger. "Now," he said flicking his fingers apart, "the fireflies are free."

"And so are they," said Vates. He motioned toward the room with his staff. "So are they."

The room grew quiet. Clunks sounded as mugs were set down. Everyone turned and looked toward Landon and his friends. After a long, somewhat uncomfortable fit of silence, they suddenly broke into applause. Hardy quickly joined in, jumping up and down and giggling.

"There's something else," Vates said loudly over the ovation. "These folks have been busy sprucing this place up!" He raised both hands until the people quieted. "Addlefoot?" he called.

A fellow near the bar hopped up onto a table. "At your service, Vates, sir!"

"What are the new passwords?"

Passwords? Landon mused. Weren't they inside the tree? Why would they need passwords in here? What was supposed to happen? As he puzzled this over, not only Addlefoot but the entire room resounded—

"Nuthatches and raspberries!"

Uh-oh. Landon reflexively clamped his hands to his ears, half-flinching in anticipation of a giant slab of tree trunk swinging open and then closing with a boom.

A section of the wall was pulling away. Actually, several pieces from the trunk were moving. They were not swinging outward, however. They were *lifting* outward like, well, like Landon imagined the doors on a spaceship would be raised outside the ship. Cool air poured in from all around. Outside, Landon could see, it was still daylight, although the air had a slightly pinkish hue to it. It must be getting toward late afternoon.

Then Landon saw shadows. They didn't bother him, however. These were normal shadows that did not move, at least not quickly or on their own. They only grew, slowly, darkening the ground from the slant of the sun beyond the treetops.

"The green," Landon said, gazing out at the wide-open space where the dome had been only hours before. Had it been only hours? Or had he been asleep (on this hard table? He hardly wanted to know) for over a day? Perhaps a couple? Well, it didn't much matter now.

A familiar figure moved across the green. Landon's heart

galloped as his trusty friend approached. *Melech.* But then Landon's heart thudded to a halt. Riding on Melech's back were two others: Holly and—

"What's he doing with her again?" Landon muttered, gripping the edge of the table. He could feel his blood pressure mounting as confusion swirled through his mind. "Holly! Get off!" Landon shouted, running from inside the trunk to the shade beneath the tree's vast canopy. "Melech! Buck him off! Ludo's on your back!"

A hand seized Landon's shoulder, and he whirled to face Hardy, who had chased after him. "Okay, Landon," Hardy said, trying to calm him. "It's okay. Ludo. . .different now."

What was going on? Was everyone going mad? Had Ludo hypnotized them all? A whoop and a shout followed by the stuttering steps of hooves close behind spun Landon around again. He was about to charge and yank Ludo down himself.

But what he saw and heard made him pause. The lanky fellow wore no top hat or coat. His orange shock of hair was thrown back as he was laughing. And Holly was giggling. And Melech was snorting and gleefully pawing the turf. It seemed a most delightful scene. Landon had to shake his head to try to think straight. Was this all part of the spell? Was he falling for Ludo's cunning charm yet again?

"Ah, Landon! Me boy, me boy!" Ludo hopped off Melech of his own accord and pranced over to Landon. Landon clenched his fists and tightened his jaw. He was about to command Ludo to stay away from his sister and Melech and—

"Me boy!" Ludo reached out and grasped Landon's shoulder. Landon winced reflexively but then noticed Ludo's grasp did not pinch or hurt at all. It felt friendly.

"No!" Landon said, twisting out from under Ludo's hand. "I won't fall for it again. You can't—"

"The Coin is gone," said Ludo plaintively. "I won't be reading it again. I did find this, however, which I would like to give you." Ludo reached into his trousers pocket. He looked rather comical, really, with windblown tufts of orange hair, green knickers, a slightly puffed and ruffled white shirt, and black shoes with silver buckles that looked too big below his scrawny ankles.

What he removed from his pocket and extended toward Landon made Landon gasp and take a step back. It was the gold fob on a gold chain. Ludo lifted it in the palm of his bony hand. He did not swing it or twirl it or dangle it before Landon's eyes.

"It is a mere token, you see, of the spell from which you have broken me. Please take it, Landon Snow. And I thank you more than you can even know."

Vates and Ditty had come up and joined Hardy behind him. Holly and Melech stood before him. And here was Ludo facing Landon and giving him a simple gold disk on a slinky chain. Landon took it, dumbfounded, and was surprised at its heaviness. After blinking stupidly at it a few times, he said, "This is real gold."

"And perfectly crafted, too," added Ludo with a smile. It wasn't that tight, nutcracker-like grin he used to brandish. It seemed a genuine smile of happiness, not a devious smirk of malice.

"And this chain," said Landon admiringly.

"The lightest and strongest of spun links, methinks." Ludo nodded.

Vates stepped close and leaned in. "And remember, both of you, before being taken in anew by its beautiful shine— that it is merely a coin on some string. It's an ornament. And may it never again be used as an instrument of torment."

Landon covered the disk with his fingers and looked up at Ludo. Even Ludo's features seemed to have softened. His nose was less pointy and his ears less sharp. His blue eyes, which always used to be narrowed in a scrutinizing squint, now widened with genuine joviality. The tautness of his face, as well as his body, seemed to have been replaced by a loose, relaxed skin. He was definitely Ludo, yet he was someone altogether changed from who he had been before.

Yes, Landon thought, agreeing with Hardy now. *He is different.*

Landon put the fob in his pocket and, after only a brief hesitation, extended his hand. When Ludo grasped it and gently shook, Landon felt a wave of relief and something akin to joy flow through his body. The sensation became so strong that he had to let go of Ludo's hand and look away before he started to cry. "Thanks," said Landon, patting his pocket. "I'll, uh, keep it." He'd meant to say he'd "treasure it" or "cherish it," but "keep" is what came out.

Holly had dismounted and, after waiting a moment outside the quiet circle, she poked her head in. "Landon," she said, sounding breathy and excited, "I want to show you something. Come with me!"

Landon glanced around at this incredible group. Melech, Ludo, Vates, Hardy, and Ditty. He nodded to each one and then said to them all, "We'll be right back." As soon as he'd said it, however, he felt a strange lump in his throat that felt heavier than the gold fob in his pocket. But he took his sister's hand as she led him back inside the tree trunk.

The valley folk were still drinking and chatting merrily among the wood tables. They hardly seemed to notice as Landon and Holly entered and walked to the stairway along the right-hand wall.

"It's up here," said Holly, pulling Landon up the solid wood stairs. They passed the opening to the branch corridor that led to the balcony with the lenses and megaphone. Fading sunlight trickled through, and Landon realized this was the first sunset at Echoing Green without the flipping of the great Coin. At least it was the first one that Landon had been awake for like this. He paused by the hollow branch hallway to appreciate the silence accompanying the fading light.

"Come on!" urged Holly. "Before it's dark. You've got to see this."

"Where are we going?" asked Landon. It suddenly struck him that the last time he'd been up here on the stairway—where it began to spiral—was when he had been coming down it from beneath the tree in the Button Up Library.

"There are higher balconies going up," said Holly. She stopped and turned, her eyes shining with excitement. "And from the top one, Landon"—she drew in a deep breath and let it out—"you can see the sea."

Landon stared back. "What? You mean, like the ocean?"

Holly nodded and smiled.

A vision popped into Landon's head of endless blue water sparkling beneath the setting sun. "Well, come on, then!" he said. "What are we waiting for?"

Holly giggled and turned and raced on up ahead of him. But as Landon chased after her, he noticed something seemed different. The stairs stopped spiraling and went up straight. And then one creaked a strange, familiar creak. By the time Landon figured out why it sounded familiar, he had already toppled over Holly, who had tripped at the top of the stairs. They both sat up and looked at each other. They were sitting on the landing atop the stairs at their grandparents' house in Button Up, Minnesota. And somebody was coming out of the bathroom at the end of the hall.

Chapter Nineteen

Bridget came padding out from the bathroom in a flannel nightgown with Winnie-the-Pooh on it. She was yawning, her mouth open wide, her eyes nearly shut, and was about to turn and enter her bedroom when she stopped. Her dark curly hair was pressed flat on one side. She stared down the hallway toward the stairs through half-shut eyes. Suddenly they flew wide open.

"Landon?" she said, walking stiffly. "Holly? What are you guys—"

"Shh!" said Landon, pressing a finger to his lips. "Is everyone else still sleeping?" He glanced warily at their parents' door. It was dark underneath.

"Yeah," Bridget said, yawning again and letting her eyes return to half-mast. "It's only. . .well. . .it's Saturday," she said. She had glanced at her wrist, which was bare, and then let the day of the week speak for itself.

Landon tried to think quickly. He was feeling very

disoriented, having just stepped up from the tree. He was sure Holly was probably feeling the same way. *Holly*—he glanced at her and smiled. He was so glad she had shared this adventure with him. Now he wouldn't have to convince her of it. Besides, she had had to be part of it. She had played an integral role in the Auctor's plan.

"Bridget," Landon said softly, "Holly and I were just tired of being so long in the dark. We're up to see the sunrise. Do you want to come with us?"

Bridget still seemed half asleep. She surprised Landon by eventually nodding and murmuring, "Yeah."

Oh, great, Landon thought. Now they really had to do it. He looked at Holly, but she still seemed in shock. "Okay," said Landon, "then go get your shoes—or boots—and your jacket and hat. It's cold out. Okay?"

Bridget made a snuffling sound and shuffled into her room. A moment later she sauntered back out, still only in her nightgown. "Downstairs," she said, yawning. "My jacket and hat."

"Oh, right," said Landon.

He and Holly stood and began walking down the steps. They stayed near the edge to avoid the creaks. Bridget came down one soft thump at a time behind them. Landon stood looking out at the darkness as Bridget slowly got her jacket, boots, and hat on. Holly stood next to Landon and eventually spoke one word.

"Wow."

Landon looked at her. "Wow, what?" he whispered.

She kept staring outside. "It's so dark and cold."

"Yes," said Landon. "But the sun's coming. I can feel it already."

"Light and warmth," said Holly quietly. "And no more shadows."

"No more shadows," Landon echoed, looking back outside. A hint of light touched the sky above the trees.

Bridget was bundled up and ready, and Landon wondered if she was even aware of what she was doing. "What are you guys talking about?" said Bridget. "What shadows?"

Before Landon could answer, a noise startled the three of them. The floor had groaned behind them, and Landon sensed someone approaching. He turned to look.

"Now what might you three be doing up so early, hmm?" Grandpa Karl stood in his bathrobe and slippers. He always seemed to be awake when things were going on inside the house.

"Hi, Grandpa," said Landon, trying to sound casual. "We're just going outside to watch the sunrise."

Grandpa Karl took a few more steps toward them. His hands were in his bathrobe pockets. "And you need a flashlight to see the sunrise, do you?" He eyed the instrument in Landon's hand suspiciously, although he seemed to be smiling beneath his gray beard.

"What?" Landon looked at his hand. "How did—?" Sure enough, there was his flashlight. He clicked the switch on and off, but nothing happened. The batteries were dead.

"And a flashlight that doesn't work at that," said Grandpa Karl. "Hmm."

Landon set the flashlight down. He looked tentatively at his grandfather. "Do you want to come, too, Grandpa?"

Grandpa Karl chuckled. "No, no. You kids go ahead. I'll watch what I can from here. It's amazing what you can see from this house sometimes. . . ."

Landon looked at him curiously. "Okay, well, we'll be outside."

"Be sure to come back for breakfast," said Grandpa Karl. "Grandma Alice always cooks up especially good meals when you and your folks are here."

The thought of breakfast made Landon's stomach growl. "We'll be right back," he said. As he stepped outside to meet the cold, crisp air, Landon realized that he had said the same thing to his friends beneath the big tree, in the other world: *We'll be right back.* It seemed his friends were still with him, too, stepping out to greet the sun with him and his sisters. Vates, Melech, Hardy, and Ludo, yes, and—

"Ditty."

"What?" Landon inhaled a gulp of icy air.

"Ditty," said Holly, her breath misting even in the darkness. "You were right. She's cute." She smiled at Landon, and he smiled back.

Their feet crunched through the hard-topped snow. Bridget seemed to be shuffling across it behind them more than breaking through. Of course, she was following in their softened footsteps.

"What are you guys talking about?" she whined. "And who's Bitty?"

Landon and Holly laughed. "Ditty," he said. "Not 'Bitty.' Perhaps you'll meet her someday."

They paused before the trees and gazed up through the bare branches. The sky turned gray and then a pale shade of pink. Landon patted a heavy disk inside his pocket and whispered to himself, "Ho, Ludo."

The rosy fingers of dawn continued to spread, drawing

away the darkness. Landon closed his eyes, took a deep breath, and smiled. It was good to feel the light on his face.

His stomach growled and Landon opened his eyes.

"Yeah," said Holly. "I'm hungry, too. How about breakfast?"

"Sounds good," said Landon.

"And then," said Bridget, pausing to let a yawn escape, "we can go sledding."

Landon and his sisters turned around to head for the house. As the snow brightened across the yard, Landon patted Bridget's shoulder. "It looks like a perfect day for sledding," he said. "Just perfect."

About the Author

R. K. (Randall Kent) Mortenson, an ordained minister in the Church of the Lutheran Brethren, has been writing poems and stories since he was a kid. *Landon Snow and the Shadows of Malus Quidam* is his second novel. Mortenson currently serves as a navy chaplain in Florida. He lives with his wife and daughter in Jacksonville.

Other books by R. K. Mortenson:

Landon Snow
and the Auctor's Riddle

Be Sure to Watch for:

Landon Snow

and the Island of Arcanum

Coming Fall 2006!